GREY MATTER

(Nothing Is Ever What It Seems)

A Novel

GREY MATTER

(Nothing Is Ever What It Seems)

A Novel

JAMES CAPUANO

2014
New Street Communications, LLC
Wickford, RI

newstreetcommunications.com

Published 2014 by
New Street Communications, LLC
Wickford, Rhode Island
newstreetcommunications.com

For Richard,

my Big Brother, who's always looking out for me;

and for Matt,

who's always there when I need him

(except for that one time).

CHAPTER ONE

Why can't everyone just leave me the fuck alone?

That was the question that was playing through John Reinhartsen, Jr's head as his brain was attempting to locate consciousness one late spring morning. It was unseasonably chilly, as evidenced by the frost on the window panes, and Johnnie had a vague recollection of being out late the night before doing nothing in particular with no one in particular.

Whenever anyone asked him what he "did", he usually said he was a writer, after which he would change the subject. If pressed to explain what he was working on he'd say (with a somewhat devious look in his eye) "it's a dark tale about an only child who kills his parents in order to inherit their substantial fortune". Nine times out of ten that ended the conversation.

Johnnie had awakened that morning in the middle of dreaming about his own parents. "Why can't everyone just leave me the fuck alone" was very much his mantra growing up and he frequently awoke with those very words on his lips. An only child, he himself had inherited a substantial fortune after his mom and dad were found dead in their Greenwich, Connecticut mansion, the apparent victims of a home invasion. At least that's what the official police report had said. Johnnie had come home from his college prep course to find his mother lying dead in her bed, a Louisville Slugger nestled beside her lifeless body; the sweet spot covered in a disconcerting mix of blood and Princeton-educated brain matter. His father, whom he didn't actually get to see, was found in the garage with both legs broken, his skull fractured, his fingers smashed and a bicycle pump shoved halfway down his throat. Johnnie didn't know he was an orphan until the police informed him of his new status in life. Fortunately, they spared him the gory details of his father's state of being. He was sixteen at the time.

He begrudgingly moved in with his aunt and uncle after his parent's gruesome departure, not because he wanted to; but because some ancient troll of a judge said he had to. Aunt Ruth and Uncle Dave also lived in Greenwich, only a few blocks away from the house Johnnie grew up in which meant that the school was the same and so were the people. Even the sunrises and sunsets were the same. Much to his surprise, the biggest change in his young life came in the form of moving from one big old house to another. Through no fault of his own he wasn't very close with his mother and father, so their sudden disappearance didn't seem to leave that big an impression on him. His aunt and uncle didn't have any children of their own and were ill-prepared to deal day in and day out with a sixteen year old whose parents had just been murdered. They were, however, fully prepared to control the considerable fortune of a sixteen year old whose parents had just been murdered until his eighteenth birthday, at which point he would have full control over the funds.

John Reinhartsen, Sr. was the Managing Partner and CEO of a mega-successful hedge fund he founded and had a well-earned reputation for being one of Wall Street's nastiest motherfuckers. If anyone or anything stood in his way, he had it removed ("removal" being a purposefully ambiguous term). Early on in his career he orchestrated such removals on his own. Later, he employed a whole host of characters who were more than happy to earn a living removing the "trash", as Big John liked to put it. He thrived on intimidating people and no one was exempt from being the target of his innate meanness. Except maybe Johnnie. He had a soft spot, albeit small, for his son in whom he saw glimpses of his own childhood. Senior, like Junior, had been a timid child who had trouble socializing and was often the target of adolescent abuse, both physical and emotional. But Big John had a funny way of expressing his grown-up feelings – funny, that is, if you consider screaming, cursing and putting your fist through walls amusing. Johnnie was terrified of his father and did his best to avoid contact with him whenever possible, often pretending to be caught up in some complicated homework assignment, or racing to put out the trash due to some unexpected garbage emergency.

Johnnie's mother Jacquie, a beautiful, well-educated woman; was a serious boozer who hated her life and just about everything attached to it, particularly Big John. She barely acknowledged little Johnnie while he was growing up other than to scream at him about one thing or another: "take a bath you disgusting little rat. Your stink repulses me". She would follow that up moments later with an affectionate "there's my handsome boy! Come give Momma a hug". Needless to say, this routine kept Johnnie so off balance he had a hard time figuring out who the real Jacqueline Reinhartsen was. It would be years before he would come to understand that one manifestation of her personality was as valid as the other; that it was okay to love her when she loved him, and to hate her when she didn't. This simple realization would give Johnnie license later on in life to love and hate with equal intensity; to have little or no concept of a middle ground.

Johnnie's Aunt Ruth considered it her birthright to be compensated in some way for the daunting task of managing her brother's sophisticated finances and looking after his son after his passing and Uncle Dave had no issue with that. In fact, Dave was more than happy to skim off the top. "Why shouldn't I wet my beak a little?" Johnnie overheard him saying on more than one occasion. "That little shit has more money than he'll ever know what to do with anyway."

The notion of caring for children never even made it as far as the bottom of Ruth and Dave's priority list and Johnnie, bright and perceptive as he was, picked up on that pretty quickly. They rarely wondered if the boy was hungry, or whether or not he was applying himself in school. More often than not they thought he was an intruder when they'd hear the door open and close, all the while forgetting he lived with them. But it would be almost two full years before he'd be able to get his hands on those funds and, until then, he'd have to suck it up and deal with his father's malevolent older sister and her functionally illiterate shit-head of a husband. The least he could do, he thought, would be to make them as miserable as possible every step of the way.

Ruth and Dave may have gotten great pleasure out of spending her brother's hard-earned cash on exotic vacations, cars and a long list of ridiculous cosmetic surgeries (Dave once had his breasts reduced the same day Ruth had hers enlarged), all the while thinking no one was the wiser. But Johnnie was determined to make good and sure their satisfaction was short-lived. 'Ol Dave would get what was coming to him sooner or later and the longer it took, Johnnie reasoned, the more pleasure he would derive from that day of reckoning. He knew to the penny what his portfolio was worth at the time of his father's demise. He'd figured out the combination to Big John's safe when he was only eight years old, having stood behind the curtain in the den with a miniature telescope Big John had brought back from some far away land, training it purposefully on his father's right hand as he hurriedly twisted and turned the safe's tumbler. He would then carefully read through all of his father's financial documents every time he was alone in the house, which was often.

He may not have understood all he was reading, but he did come to learn that in addition to the mountains of cash held in the accounts, he also owned tens of millions of dollars' worth of municipal and treasury bonds. His father was not one to gamble in complicated financial products (which bore much risk and which he pushed his employees to aggressively market to less sophisticated investors), or, for that matter, the myriad of Silicon Valley start-ups that were destined to fail according to Big John's investment philosophies.

But he did have an affinity for scooping up real estate and personally owned hundreds of thousands of acres in the Caribbean, Asia and the western portion of the United States. Johnnie would sit and imagine visiting all those properties wearing an expensive, hand-made business suit and carrying a finely carved, immaculately polished walking stick – the quintessential land baron – informing those that occupied the space that rent was due "on the first of the month, and not a day later". It was a line from some movie he'd seen and he couldn't wait to try it out on actual people.

CHAPTER TWO

Brendan McAvoy, also sixteen years old at the time of Big John and Jacquie's passing, lived in Darien, Connecticut; a picturesque New England village and home to the upper-upper class and their privileged offspring, much like Johnnies home town. Brendan's dad, Tom, worked for Big John and was a Partner and Chief Operating Officer at the firm.

Tom was not at all like Big John, save for the fact that he liked money and all the spoils that came along with such fantastic wealth. He, his wife Laura and Brendan often socialized with the Reinhartsen's, but it was more out of a sense of obligation than the product of a close friendship. Tom didn't much like Big John; didn't at all approve of his lack of ethics and generally nasty demeanour – the antithesis of what made Tom "Tom". But, he rationalized: sometimes you have to sacrifice your own standards a little bit for the greater good, which in this case meant Laura and Brendan - and his own egotistical fascination with status and wealth.

Tom and Laura still liked each other well enough. They had a cordial, if distant relationship and neither one ever raised their voices in confrontation. Whether that was out of a sense of not wishing to upset Brendan or the fact that neither of them cared to confront one another about anything any more was a mystery – one they were happy to leave unsolved. It hadn't always been that way, of course. Back when they were kids, every moment spent apart found Laura struggling to breathe; and Tom behaving as though he'd lost a limb. But they truly loved Brendan in their own way. Tom had a particular affinity for the boy, spending as much of his free time as he could with him, coaching his little league and soccer teams and taking him for long walks in the woods where he was delighted to pass on his hard earned wisdom about life, love and the pursuit of happiness to his only child.

Laura had a very difficult time conceiving and she and Tom tried everything money could buy to do so, but with little success. And then one day, after years of heartache, disappointment and a diminishing belief that they'd ever actually become parents, they'd gotten the news they'd been waiting for: Laura was pregnant. "All those years of prayer and sacrifice must have paid off; this is nothing less than a miracle!" Tom happily exclaimed to his wife after she shared the good news with him.

Brendan coasted through the first sixteen years of his life. He was a good-looking, likeable kid who fit in comfortably with everyone around him. He was a jock and an "A" student and was quite adept at manoeuvring between the two. He'd won his school's high-dive championship two years in a row and was a starting pitcher on the baseball team, leading them to their first championship season in over two decades.

His life of privilege was tempered only by his father's constant reminder that he was obliged to help the less fortunate any way he could, whenever he could. It was his responsibility to "give back". The shoe could very easily be on the other foot one day and he would certainly hope to have someone looking after him if, God forbid, that ever became the case. Brendan understood this intuitively.

Johnnie, on the other hand, couldn't have been more different. With his parents gone and his "caregivers" not caring the least bit about what he was up to, Johnnie was on his own, left to his own devices. This was not good. Johnnie's moral compass, along with the will to succeed, had been stepped on and cracked when he was a child and no one ever bothered to repair it. Big John and Jacquie were too caught up in their own little dramas to even notice that Johnnie was shifting dangerously off course, which resulted in Johnnie drifting even further away.

He dropped out of high school the end of his junior year – a few short months after his parent's demise - and dedicated himself to smoking the best weed money could buy. Johnnie was incredibly stoned throughout most of his waking hours. Needless to say, he lacked the motivation to do anything other than walk to the deli a few blocks away to pick up some munchies. He had the complexion of his aunt's living room drapes and neither she nor his uncle ever bothered to take notice.

This pattern would escalate over the next two years until his eighteenth birthday finally arrived, at which point he would bid his aunt and uncle a fond fuck you and move to New York City, land of concrete and crime. He finally had control over his own financial destiny and was keenly aware that, although he had more than enough wealth to sustain him through the rest of his life, the cash portion of his holdings had shrunk noticeably – the result, no doubt, of his guardian's more than occasional "tastings".

While pretending to oversee and finance a comfortable existing for their poor, orphaned nephew, the dirty old bastards were busy living it up! And with *his* money! Not that it really mattered. Big John's other investments had increased substantially enough over that period to cover a good portion of the deficit, but Johnnie was not inclined to let his aunt and uncle off the hook for pilfering those funds. Yet he would continue to bide his time. It would be worth the wait, he assured himself. He had nothing better to do anyway.

He hooked himself up with a spectacular 2 bedroom, 2 ½ bath apartment on the upper-west side of Manhattan, having purchased it with cash, several million dollars' worth, and furnished it with the help of Pottery Barn and Restoration Hardware. He had amazing views of both the park and the south-eastern skyscrapers that dotted the city's skyline. He longed for nothing and desired even less.

He had gotten himself to the point where comfortably numb was a natural state of being and he would easily sustain that wondrous condition with the aid of several pounds of premium marijuana he kept in a special humidor he had built into his walk-in bedroom closet, which just so happened to be about the size of most studio apartments in Manhattan. He'd informed his architect that he was a cigar aficionado, an attribute inherited from his late father, and that it was of the utmost importance that his humidor comes equipped with a disaster recovery mechanism containing its own power supply.

This was a critical requirement as he would not be able to live with himself should he allow his deceased father's priceless Cuban cigars, collected over the course of a grown-up lifetime, to dry out and become stale. The architect, a cigar enthusiast himself, understood and quickly assuaged Johnnie's concerns as only a professional could – sharing with him in painstaking detail the intricate algorithms of the humidor's computerized control system. As far as Johnnie was concerned he needed nothing from anyone and owed society even less.

Then he met Hayley.

Hayley Mullany was a 22 year-old painter possessing a slightly off-kilter nose and a silvery, hairline scar beneath her right earlobe that offset her striking beauty just enough to make her approachable. While she did sell the occasional painting now and then, she never-the-less found it necessary to work evenings in order to make ends meet. She maintained a tiny studio apartment in the city that had a northern exposure which provided consistent, natural light throughout the day – perfect for a starving artist who couldn't afford to rent a separate studio with proper lighting in order to pursue her calling.

They met while the two of them were wandering through Central Park one sunny morning, lost in their own little worlds. Hayley was talking on her cell phone, oblivious to her surroundings; Johnnie was smoking a joint, enjoying a perfect sense of harmony with his. They walked directly into each other while circling the Alice in Wonderland fountain and Hayley's cell phone flew out of her hand, coming to rest on the outside ledge of the sculpture. Johnnie, thinking nothing of it, stepped right into the chilly water without missing a beat to retrieve the phone, which, if the coy little smile on her face were any indication, Hayley found very endearing. As Johnnie turned to walk away Hayley grabbed him by the arm: "Hey, I'm sorry about that. I wasn't paying attention to where I was going. Would've really sucked to lose my iPhone for the third time this year. Thanks for rescuing it. That was very noble of you."

Johnnie, not knowing how to respond to this lovely woman's admiration, whether real or contrived, did what came naturally to him – he offered her a toke, which she gladly partook of.

They sat down on a nearby bench, passing the joint back and forth without uttering a word until Hayley finally broke the silence. "Holy shit! This pot is incredible! Can I buy a couple of joints off of ya?"

"Well, I'm no drug dealer, but I'll twist you up a few, on the house."

"Wow, a real-life gentleman. First you rescue my phone, braving the knee-deep water; then you supply me with the ingredients to inspire me. I'm an artist, by the way. Water colors. I usually paint landscapes but I'm getting bored with that. I need to head in a different direction before I give up on painting altogether. What do you do?"

"I'm a writer" Johnnie replied.

"No way!" responded Hayley. "Have you written anything I might have read?"

"Probably not" Johnnie answered dryly. "Have you painted anything I might have seen", Johnnie asked.

"No, but fortunately for me, I'm also an excellent stripper, so I do OK financially."

"How'd you get to be a stripper?" Johnnie wanted to know, his interest level soaring from 60 to 120 mph before she even had a chance to finish the sentence.

"A girlfriend of mine from high school turned me on to it", Hayley informed him. "Once she mentioned she was bringing home upwards of three thousand a week, cash, the decision pretty much made itself. Men are such suckers. Wiggle your ass in their face and grind on them a little and they practically hand over their ATM cards. So, Mr. Writer, what are you writing about?"

"It's a dark tale about a young boy, an only child, who kills his parents in order to inherit their substantial fortune."

"Wow, that *is* dark. Does he get away with it?"

"I'm still not sure how it ends", Johnnie replied.

"How old are you, anyway?" Hayley asked.

"Twenty two" Johnnie lied. "Why do you ask?"

"Just curious. You're kinda cute. Wanted to see if you were in my age range. You never know."

"You never know what?" asked Johnnie.

"You never know anything, really", replied Hayley.

CHAPTER THREE

Shortly after his sixteenth birthday, prior to Big John and Jacquie's demise, Laura sat Brendan down for a private chat while Tom was out running errands one Saturday morning. "Brendan, honey; come sit. There's something I need to talk to you about", she said while doing her best to fabricate a smile.

"What's up mom? I was just on my way out to practice", Brendan told her.

"Brendan, I have something to tell you that's not going to be easy for you to hear, so I'm just going to come right out and say it", Laura went on. "A long time ago, I made a terrible decision", she said. After an interminable pause, she continued. "Many years ago, before you were born, I gave in to a temptation that altered the course of our family's lives."

"Mom, I don't know where this is going, but I don't want to hear anymore", Brendan informed Laura. "I don't need to know all about our fucked-up family history."

"Please don't curse, honey", she continued. "And you do need to hear this. I just can't keep it to myself any longer and it's not something your father can know about. Not *Ever. OK?*"

"Now I *definitely* don't want to hear this", he said emphatically. "I've got to run. I'm gonna be late."

"Many years ago, before you were born", she went on, ignoring her sons pleas; "I had a 'relationship' with your dad's boss, John Reinhartsen. I became pregnant as a result of that relationship. Brendan, Tom McAvoy is not your biological father. John Reinhartsen is. But please don't tell your dad any of this – it would destroy him. He loves you more than anything on this earth. You know, it's funny; I can't truly say I regret what happened. Your dad and I tried for years to become pregnant but his sperm was too slow. If I hadn't done what I'd done, I wouldn't have you, and that would be far harder for me to live with than the horrible guilt I've awakened to each morning for the past seventeen years. Brendan - please keep this between us and know that your dad and I love you, no matter what."

"*Are you fucking kidding me?*" Brendan shot back. "Why the *fuck* would you share something like that with me. Why the *fuck* would I need to know that???"

"Brendan, please. The cursing!" was all Laura said.

"Jesus Christ, mom! You lay something like that on me and your only concern is that I'm fucking *cursing*??" Brendan said, shocked. "Seriously, what the fuck is wrong with you?"

"Sweetheart, I'm your mother and I won't have you talking to me that way!" was all Laura could say.

"Are you sure Jacquie Reinhartsen isn't my mother?" he said in as nasty a tone as he could muster. "I mean, *anything's* possible at this point, wouldn't you say, *Laura*?"

With that he stormed out of the house, leaving his mother to contemplate the magnitude of her most recent bad decision. What neither of them had realized was that Tom had come in through the back door and was standing in the kitchen, listening to every word. Ironically, Tom already new about the affair. He had followed Big John and Laura on several occasions and watched as they went into the Pierre Hotel, laughing playfully. Tom would sit across the street in the park and wait for them to emerge, always looking smug and satisfied. What he didn't know for sure but always suspected was that Big John had fathered his son, Brendan. But hearing Laura actually say the words knocked him off balance. It triggered something foreign in him. It turned his whole world upside down.

Brendan sat on the bleachers behind home plate with his hands in his jacket pocket and his thoughts on Big John Reinhartsen. The expression on his face betrayed what he was thinking: there was just no way that motherfucker would be allowed to get away with what he did. Period. If there's a God, Big John would get his.

Tom was right – it *was* Brendan's responsibility to help the less fortunate. And in this particular instance, Brendan contemplated; Tom - his real dad, the one he loved and admired - *was* the "less fortunate". Now he needed to figure out just how he was going to "give back".

Hayley grew up in the city in a huge housing development called Stuyvesant Town on the east side. Her dad was a fire fighter and her mom a 4th grade teacher in the local public school on east 20th street. The product of a strict Irish-Catholic upbringing, Hayley attended the Immaculate Conception grammar school on East 14th street along with her two older brothers and three older sisters, all born within a year or so of each other, and went to church every Sunday with her family. She lived a normal, happy childhood; had an army of friends and prayed to God every night, thanking him for giving her such a wonderful life. And then the unimaginable happened.

The doorbell rang one morning at 4 a.m. as the family slept peacefully. Hayley's mom attempted to calm all six children down as they ran to the front door. As she opened the door they immediately recognized the captain of their dad's battalion, Tim Brady; and the fire chaplain, Monsignor Francis Costello. Both wore a sombre expression.

"No" Theresa Mullany exclaimed with a sigh. "Please God; let this be a bad dream."

"We're so terribly sorry, Theresa" Captain Brady uttered. "It was a 4-alarmer and Bill went in to pull out a woman and child even though he was told not to until we had that sector of the building secured. He just couldn't stand by and watch even though he knew exactly what the risk was. He put his breathing apparatus on the 6 year old boy, got the boy and his mother out of the building safely but unfortunately succumbed to smoke inhalation himself shortly thereafter. He's a hero, your husband and father is. You should all be very proud."

But proud was not at all what Theresa and the kids were feeling at that moment. As the family stood there, not knowing what to do next, Hayley, who was eight years old at the time, made the decision she could no longer be friends with God.

As Johnnie turned the key and opened the door to his apartment Hayley stood behind him, taking in the scenery. "Fuck me! How does an unemployed writer afford to live in a place like this?"

"Who said I was unemployed?" Johnnie noted. "How do you know I'm not a successful Wall Street hedge fund guy making a bundle of money?"

"Are you?" asked Hayley curiously.

"Nah, but I coulda been. Frankly, I'm a bit insulted."

"Settle down tiger, my bad. I mean, I just kinda figured if you were roaming around Central Park on a random Tuesday morning in jeans and sneakers, smoking a fattie, you were unemployed."

"I'm just fuckin' with you. I *am* unemployed. I live off a pretty sweet trust fund my grandfather left me though. If all goes well, I'll never have to put in an honest day's work in my life", Johnnie casually informed the hard-working stripper / artist. "Anyway, let me roll up those numbers for you. Make yourself at home while I do.

Want a drink or something?" Johnnie offered, not quite recognizing his own voice as the words were coming out of his mouth. The last time Johnnie allowed himself to engage in this much conversation with a fellow human being was, well, never.

When he came back into the living room Hayley was standing at the window.

"I see you checking me out through the reflection, you know", Hayley said. "You like what you see?" she asked facetiously.

"What's not to like?" Johnnie answered, slightly embarrassed as he handed Hayley six tightly rolled joints. "This shit is extra potent so just take a hit or two at a time 'til you figure out your tolerance level – I don't need you freaking out on me."

"Torch one of those bad boys up, Mary. I'll be the judge of how much I can tolerate" Hayley commented, wryly.

Johnnie, uncharacteristically, did as he was instructed to do. The two of them, strangers not more than 45 minutes ago, were on the verge of taking their buzz to the next level, chatting away non-stop as they polished off the joint. As he flicked the roach out of his 20th story window he realized he hadn't eaten all day. Of course, there was nothing in the house that was edible, so he suggested they go get some food. "There's a great burger place a coupla blocks away?" Johnnie offered.

"I don't eat meat", replied Hayley.

"What's wrong with eating meat?" Johnnie asked with a hint of a chuckle.

"Nothing, if you're a lion, or possibly a T. Rex, I suppose" Hayley shot back. "But I'm a vegan. I've read all about the inhumane treatment at slaughter-houses and cattle farms and I, for one, want nothing to do with it."

"Really?" Johnnie replied with mock-astonishment. "I'm assuming you know that the word 'humane' is derived from the word 'human'. Did you also know it's been scientifically proven that cattle and all the other varieties of *meat* that are available for purchase on the open market do not possess the linguistic capabilities, deep thoughts or tool making skills that would qualify them as being 'human'? So it stands to reason that, although we as human beings are perfectly capable of treating fellow human beings 'inhumanely', it's not realistic to apply that same definition and intent when referring to the management of our food supply."

"That's impressive, but it's also bullshit", Hayley replied with both a hint of anger and a touch of respect in her voice. This guy was more on the ball than she'd initially given him credit for. "Are you telling me that you think it's ok for these industries to treat animals with complete and utter indifference, with no regard whatsoever for their emotional or physical well-being, just because they eventually show up on our dinner plates and ultimately get shit out of our asses?"

"That's not at all what I'm saying, although that is an interesting way of looking at it. You, yourself, just said it's ok to feast on meat if you're a lion or a dinosaur. Well, have you ever watched those nature shows where you get to see lions and other predators hunting for their next meal? Where you get to watch in super-slow motion as a lioness – the female of the species, by the way –seeks out and isolates the weakest member from the rest of the herd, usually a sick baby animal, and proceeds to rip it apart with her sharp teeth and claws so her own babies can get the nourishment they need to survive? Nothing 'humane' about that scene, I would say. What makes it ok for lesser animals to act savagely in order to survive but not ok for the same rules to apply to human beings?"

"What makes it not ok is the fact that human beings have 'evolved' by the grace of God to be moral and kind and sympathetic, not to mention extremely intelligent – in some cases, anyway – and should know better than to treat other living creatures so callously", Hayley countered.

"Oh, really?" Johnnie responded. "And that was decreed by whom, God Himself? Do you really believe "God" created human beings in his image and bestowed upon them the virtues of morality, kindness and sympathy? That he woke up one day and decided 'all these other animals kinda suck, I'd better create something more substantial'. How naïve can you be? Isn't it more likely that morality, kindness and sympathy are the result of the painstaking process of evolution as well? That we developed these characteristics over time in order to give our species a better chance to survive as opposed to wiping ourselves off the face of the earth, which might still happen anyway? I say it's our evolutionary right to eat a burger any time we feel like it. Just because we were able to figure out more efficient ways to ensure our food supply and not starve doesn't mean we should be penalized for it. You think a lioness living on the African savannah wouldn't be ecstatic to have someone tossing her 100 pounds of meat every other day rather than having to expend the energy to chase it down herself? "

"I'm not the one who's being naïve, Johnnie Boy. Besides, there's no reason to eat meat nowadays, anyway. We can survive perfectly well on vegetables, fruits and nuts which, by the way, do not undergo hideous slaughter rituals in order to end up on the dining room table. Not to mention; veggies, fruits and nuts don't have *emotions*, or a *soul,* and they don't experience *pain.*"

"And you know this because you were a head of lettuce in a previous life?" Johnnie countered. "How could you possibly say that with such certainty? How do you know an apple doesn't experience pain when it's picked off a tree? If you disconnect an apple from its food source and let it sit for a few days, it rots. That apple was once alive and growing, and now it's dead. Why can't one assume that it might have felt something as it 'died' or was picked off the tree? Whether pain, pleasure or indifference. How the fuck can we possibly know?"

"You know what? I think we're both way too stoned to make any sense at this point. Why don't we agree to disagree for now, get naked and make each other feel really good about being alive" said Hayley.

Johnnie, stubborn and inexperienced as he was with women, didn't even pick up on Hayley's generous offer. "I just need to make a couple 'a more points. I'll make it quick – I promise. First off, I completely disagree with your statement that 'we don't need to eat meat anyway'. The only reason we're able to have this conversation to begin with is because our ancestors were carnivorous. Meat is jam-packed with protein and calories. And without the introduction of a consistent source of high volume protein and calories into our diet, our brains never could have evolved the way they did to enable us to become the dominant species on the planet. So if you like being human, with deep thoughts and a big heart, you can thank our ancestors for developing a taste for meat. Of course there were other factors that came into play as well, but a protein-rich, high calorie diet was a key differentiator. And then there's your comment about morality, kindness and sympathy. Do you really think that "God" gave us those attributes because he wanted us to be just like him? Because a strong argument can be made for the fact that God, if he actually does exist, has had more than a little trouble living up to those lofty standards himself."

"When I was younger, much younger, I did believe that, yes. But then something horrible happened and I haven't been able to bring myself to look kindly upon the 'Creator' ever since", Hayley replied with a sadness in her voice.

"What happened to make you feel this way?" Johnnie asked sincerely.

"What happened was my dad, a fireman and the best person I've ever known, was allowed to die after inhaling too much smoke while rescuing a mother and her six year old child from a burning building. Up until that point I thought God was full of love and kindness. But how could someone who is full of love and kindness allow such a horrible thing to happen? To this day I can't figure it."

Johnnie took it all in as though he was realizing for the first time that other human beings experienced pain and sadness, too. "Wow, that's some heavy shit. I'm sorry you had to deal with that. But I can kind of relate", Johnnie said, suddenly finding himself in uncharted territory. Never had he opened up this much to anyone, let alone a beautiful woman. But he pushed forward to the best of his ability, awkwardly trying to find his stride in those new shoes he was wearing. "My parents never should have been allowed to reproduce to begin with – they were so fucked up. And I could never figure out why God would give *me* to *them*, so I guess I just stopped trying. They're both dead now, anyway. After they died I was forced to live with my father's sister and her husband and that was an even worse experience. I disappeared as soon as I was old enough to get control of my trust fund. I've just been bumming around ever since. Still struggling to recover, I guess."

Hayley, completely absorbed in the moment, leaned in and kissed Johnnie gently on the mouth. He smiled as he watched her slowly undress and push him down onto the bed. Johnnie's only thought at that moment was "thank you, God"; in utter contradiction to his own previous assertions.

Two years after the deaths of Big John and Jacquie, Brendan was still struggling to come to terms with his reality TV-like existence when a thought popped into his head, one that curiously had never occurred to him before. If Big John was his biological father that meant Johnnie was his biological half-brother. Another unexpected curve, but Brendan was seeing the ball more clearly now. On this pitch he would keep his head down and his weight back. On this pitch he would make solid contact.

It's not that he didn't like Johnnie; it's just that he could never quite figure him out – the two were so different. They knew each other well enough from all the socializing their families did when they were younger, but they were never able to connect on any significant level. Not that it mattered much to either of them.

But now things were different. Now there were some good reasons for the two to get to know each other better, not the least of which was the fact that Brendan, being the biological son of Big John Reinhartsen, felt he was entitled to a significant portion of Johnnie's inheritance.

At 2:00 a.m. the phone started ringing in Johnnie's apartment. Johnnie was in the middle of a dream in which his mother, her head crushed in and bloody after being cracked open by the baseball bat, was yelling at him to help her find her fucking brains; that it would be a terrible waste to leave such a well-educated mind scattered all over the bedroom floor. In one of those freaky instances where dream reality meets waking reality, his mother started yelling at him to answer the God-damned phone. As he was reaching out to put a chunk of grey matter back inside his mother's skull, Hayley was reaching out to shake him awake. "Johnnie, the phone. Get the phone", Hayley was whispering.

He jumped out of bed, thoroughly confused, and stood staring at Hayley, not quite sure who she was. "Mom?" Johnnie wondered out loud.

"Johnnie, answer that. It might be important" Hayley insisted.

"Who the fuck is this?" Johnnie yelled into the phone, all the while staring at Hayley. "It's two in the goddamn morning."

"Is this John Reinhartsen, Jr. from Greenwich?" the voice asked.

"Who the fuck is askin'?" Johnnie shot back.

"Just an old friend" the voice replied, after which Johnnie heard a click and a dial tone.

"Who was that?" asked Hayley.

"I have no fucking idea" said Johnnie. "That was very strange."

"Well come back to bed. Now that we're both awake….." Hayley whispered, suggestively.

CHAPTER FOUR

It was easy enough for Brendan to reach Johnnie on his cell phone given that he'd had the same number since he was eight years old. Brendan had copied it into his iPhone's contact folder one day when Johnnie wasn't paying attention for the sole purpose of making prank phone calls. He'd have Nancy Toner, the neighborhood hottie, leave him messages about how sexy he was, and how she couldn't wait for them to hook up. Whenever he'd run across Nancy after receiving the first of several such messages, Johnnie would immediately get an erection and turn the other way, red-faced and mortified. But Nancy was kind to Johnnie during those encounters, throwing out the casual "Hey Johnnie, looking good" in order to put him at ease. Of course it had the opposite effect; forcing the remaining blood in his system to flow directly to his woody, leaving him on the brink of passing out.

Finding Johnnie's new address wasn't as easy to come by however. It was a matter of trial and error. After hours of fiddling around with inane search criteria on the internet, it finally dawned on Brendan to check for recent real estate purchases and rentals under Johnnie's name within a 50 mile radius. He'd heard through the grapevine that Johnnie had finally assumed control of his inheritance and left his aunt and uncle's house for greener pastures. He'd located half a dozen promising leads and copied the addresses into his iPhone. On one occasion during his early reconnaissance missions he'd found himself in the South Bronx, knocking on the door of a 6' 4", 260 lb. "John Reinhartsen" of Columbian decent who was kind enough to explain that if he didn't "get the fuck out of his mother-fucking face immediately", he'd be swallowing one of the many 9-millemeter bullets he'd just loaded into his *pistola.*" On another occasion, he was invited into the abode of one "Juanita Reinhartsen", a Puerto Rican transvestite who told him she'd be more than happy to help him find "his little friend" if he'd just give her a second to freshen up. He'd figured that the sixth and final address in his phone had to be the one he was looking for, so he scouted out a nice perch on the west side of Central Park, right across from Johnnie's building, and settled in. It was pretty well camouflaged by the late spring growth, not that Johnnie would have noticed him anyway. The air was still chilly and the ground moist from the recent snow melt, but Brendan was prepared. He wore his Timberlands and his Patagonia down coat thinking he might be entrenched for a while. As it turned out, he got lucky. He spotted Johnnie and Hayley the moment they walked out of the building, arm in arm, only a couple of hours later.

"Wow" thought Brendan. "That freak actually landed himself a hot little girlfriend." He followed them from about a block away and watched as they went into a diner on Broadway. As he walked by he shot a quick glance through the window in order to make sure he'd cornered the right prey. Satisfied with his detective work, Brendan waited in front of a deli on the other side of the avenue until the two emerged from the diner half an hour later, still arm in arm, laughing and looking quite pleased with themselves.

"Motherfucker won't be laughing very long", Brendan thought to himself.

Ruth and Dave were happy to be rid of Johnnie but found themselves in a bit of a predicament now that he was gone. With John Jr. controlling his own finances, Ruth and Dave were shut out. There was no way their modest retirement income was going to provide them with the unrealistic lifestyle they'd grown accustomed to while "managing" Johnnie's portfolio. They were barely able to afford upkeep on the house. With a large tax payment looming, Ruth had no choice but to reach out to Johnnie for help.

"Please John", Ruth whined. "We're quite late as it is and we've received several notices that if we don't make this next payment by the end of the month we'll lose the house. Uncle Dave is not in the best of health and we'd have nowhere to go. It's only $12,000 but we simply can't afford it. Can't you please help us, Johnnie? PLEASE? After all, we did take you in and care for you after that terrible incident with your parents."

"Oh my God, Aunt Ruth, I had no idea! That's terrible. I would have thought with all that cash you and your idiot husband stole from my account over the past two years that you'd have plenty of money to make ends meet. How about this – why don't the two of you go fuck yourselves? And, while you're at it, lose my fucking number."

Johnnie hung up the phone and smiled to himself. "Goddamn, that felt *so* good" he uttered aloud. Fuck them, he thought. They made their bed, now they can die a miserable death in it for all he cared.

Uncle Dave; condescending, nasty, greedy Uncle Fucking Dave, bumped into one of the many storage boxes that cluttered the living room as he was carrying another box out to the truck. "That ungrateful son-of-a-bitch", Dave screamed to Ruth. "He couldn't dip into his millions and pay the God-damned tax bill for us? We can't even afford to hire movers and he's living it up in the city somewhere. He's just like his old man – selfish and arrogant. Well, your brother got his in the end and I'm sure that little bastard of a son will get it one day, too."

"My *brother* bought us this house. And he supported us the whole time he was around" argued Ruth. "If you weren't such a lazy son-of-a-bitch and did a better job earning, we wouldn't be in this mess today. My brother certainly had his faults but he always did right by us."

"Oh, so now the mighty John Reinhartsen is a saint in heaven", mocked Dave. "He was mean and nasty and he got what he had coming to him."

"I swear, I don't know how I've put up with you all these years", Ruth retorted. "If you weren't hung like a God-damned horse I'd have left you a long time ago."

"Ha! You got that right, sister! Now pick up those boxes and load them into the truck. I'm gonna sit down and smoke the last of my hand-rolled, Cuban cigars as I watch the sun set from my back porch one last time."

Johnnie, in his eagerness to make his aunt and uncle suffer, willingly forfeited millions of dollars when he let the county repossess the house. He knew from studying his father's financial documents that Old Dave and Ruth's house was actually his. When Big John bought the place for his sister, he had the deed made out in his name. This doubly-fucked Dave and Ruth because they couldn't even withdraw a lousy twelve grand from a home equity line to pay the county tax because it wasn't their money. "What goes around, motherfuckers", Johnnie said out loud while watching with great pleasure from a block away as his aunt and uncle struggled to load up the truck. For Johnnie it was worth letting a few million dollars slip away just to see those sons of bitches squirm.

Hayley's apartment was smaller than expected, with easels, paint pallets and unfinished landscapes in various stages of framing smothering one half of the room; while a tiny kitchenette, bathroom and futon couch occupied the other half.

"Nice place", Johnnie offered. "And conveniently designed – you can shit, scramble eggs and paint, all at the same time."

"That's pretty funny", Hayley replied sarcastically. "You know, not everyone has a 'pretty sweet trust fund' to live off of. Some of us actually have to work."

"Well if you play your cards right, you never know", said Johnnie.

"You never know what?" asked Hayley.

"You never know anything, really." replied Johnnie.

"I've heard that somewhere before. Confucius, maybe?" said Hayley.

"Let's not get carried away. Once that shit goes to your head no one ever takes you seriously anymore", lectured Johnnie.

"Do you take me seriously, Johnnie?" Hayley inquired.

"As compared to what?" he wanted to know.

"Compared to other woman you've slept with, I suppose" said Hayley.

"You 'suppose' an awful lot", said Johnnie. "You really should get behind the things you say."

"I guess it's my fear of rejection" Hayley replied. "Now, take off your clothes and get on the futon", Hayley instructed.

"Are you gonna have your way with me again, Miss H? Because I don't know if I can handle another blissful pounding", Johnnie admitted.

"Oh, I'm gonna have my way with you alright, but probably not in the way you're thinking", Hayley corrected him. She set up her easel, smeared some colors on a pallet, extracted an array of fan blenders, bristle brights and sable rounds from her brush case and got to work.

"Now lay perfectly still Johnnie, and don't move a muscle until I tell you to or I won't give you your special treat" Hayley further instructed.

Once again Johnnie did exactly as he was told to do.

Brendan, happy to be away from the sleaze-bag motel he was camping out in, decided he'd get to the diner Johnnie and Hayley ate at most mornings a few minutes ahead of them. He assumed correctly from his earlier stake-outs that it was part of their regular routine to get there around 11 am each day. So he sat in a booth with his back to the door, all the while keeping a close eye on the floor to ceiling mirror covering the wall in front of him. As he was about halfway through his western omelette he glanced up and saw Johnnie's reflection as he sat down in the booth directly behind him. Hayley was nowhere to be seen. He heard Johnnie order a double espresso with a shot of Sambuca and a side of OJ. "Pretentious motherfucker", Brendan thought.

Brendan steeled his nerves, took a deep breath and got up to use the bathroom. As he turned to exit the booth he and Johnnie made eye contact for the first time, but Johnnie just looked away as if he had no idea who Brendan was. On the way back from the bathroom, Brendan stopped in front of Johnnie's booth and spoke up: "Holy shit! John Reinhartsen! I thought that was you. What the fuck are you doing in NYC?"

"Brendan McAvoy. It's been a while" Johnnie replied with little enthusiasm.

"Sure has", said Brendan. "Last time I saw you was right after your parent's funeral. You went into hiding after that. So sorry about that, Bro. How you holdin' up anyway?" Brendan asked, as though he meant it.

"Been ok. Moved to the city recently. Needed to get away from my aunt and uncle. What about you?" Johnnie asked, although he wasn't really interested in the answer.

"Why don't I cop a squat and we can catch up a little bit", Brendan suggested. Johnnie reluctantly agreed. "I just graduated from good 'ol Darien High and still living at home. Came to the city to look for work before I go off to school. Can't go to Georgetown without some cash in my pocket", replied Brendan.

"Georgetown, huh?" Johnnie said, once again feigning interest. "Not too shabby."

"Nope, not at all. Got a free ride. Baseball scholarship", Brendan said, with just a hint of pride in his voice.

"I guess all that jock shit paid off", Johnnie said. "Well, good to see you. Take it easy."

"Slow down, Broseph. You and I go back a long ways" Brendan reminded him. "Why not hang for another minute?" Brendan suggested.

"Not interested", Johnnie replied without hesitation. "See ya."

"Come on, man. I never even got to tell you how sorry I was about what happened to Big John and Jacquie. That had to be rough" Brendan pushed. "Cops ever figure out what happened?"

"You must have read all about it. It was in all the papers", Johnnie pushed back.

"Yeah, I guess. A lot of people thought there was more to it from what I remember", said Brendan, attempting to keep Johnnie engaged.

"Couldn't care less either way", Johnnie casually replied. "They were miserable sons of bitches. Used to dream about killing them myself."

"Yeah, well; a lot of people thought you did, I wasn't one of them though", Brendan assured him.

"Oh, no? What makes you so different?" Johnnie asked.

"You were way too much of a pussy to ever go that far", Brendan answered.

"So you wanted to sit down with me so you could fire off insults? Go fuck yourself, Brendan", Johnnie shot back.

"Take it easy, Bro. I mean, I remember when we were kids. Big John and Jacquie were always up your ass about some stupid shit. You always just took it. I never even heard you answer back", Brendan reminded Johnnie.

"I used to, but it never got me anywhere. I guess I just stopped trying after a while" Johnnie said.

"Yeah, like I said", Brendan replied.

"Again with the fucking insults. You know what? I'm just gonna get up and go before I smack you."

Johnnie had had enough of the reminiscing game. And he was more than a little suspicious of why Brendan had just shown up out of the blue like that. He remembered Brendan being a sneaky motherfucker when they were kids. Always up to something, and usually at someone else's expense.

"Hey, mind if I tag along? I've got nothing going on 'til later this afternoon anyway", Brendan pleaded.

"Yeah, I do mind", Johnnie said. "I don't see you for two fucking years then you just pop up outta nowhere and start leaching onto me like a little bitch. What the fuck, Brendan?"

With that, Johnnie got up and left Brendan sitting alone in the booth. It dawned on Brendan that he probably should have formulated some sort of plan before embarking on this reconnaissance mission, but he wasn't thinking very clearly when he left his home in Connecticut. The news about Big John and his ancestry really fucked him up. He was reacting blindly, his only goal to hurt someone back. And who better than the son of that motherfucker Big John Reinhartsen?

CHAPTER FIVE

Tom and Laura were like strangers these days. They barely spoke and generally stayed in their own little domains within their massive home. Laura could feel things were different between them now. She wasn't quite sure what led to this void in communication but she wasn't entirely surprised. Tom had been much less attentive to her these past few weeks, that was obvious, but she chose not to make an issue of it. He, on the other hand, was finally letting his emotions out. After hearing Laura explain to Brendan that Big John was his father and keeping his frustration and dissatisfaction locked up for years he was finally starting to deal with the problem. But Tom wasn't the confrontational type. He preferred the passive-aggressive approach, needling away at Laura every chance he got.

"When's the boy coming home", Tom asked his wife as she was passing through his den one evening, startling her.

"He didn't say. Hopefully he'll find a job and get a feel for what it's like to have to earn your own money before going away to school", Laura informed him.

"What hotel is he staying in? I feel bad I didn't get to see him before he left. Work's been brutal. Goddamn SEC." Tom blurted out.

"You know, he really didn't say." Laura replied. "And I was so busy setting up for the Historical Society Centennial celebration that I forgot to even ask. Guess we're not winning that "Parents of the Year" award any time soon.

"That goes without say." Tom replied, a little too quickly. "What hotel do you *think* he'd be staying in? You must have some idea. Do you know of any inexpensive hotels in the city, or are you just familiar with the expensive ones", Tom asked.

"What's that supposed to mean", Laura answered, defensively. "Why would I know anything about expensive hotels in the city?" Laura asked, nervously.

"I was only asking", Tom said. "No need to be so defensive."

"I'm not being defensive", Laura replied, finding her footing. "That's just a weird question for you to ask."

"Is it?" Tom wondered. "Ha, I guess it is. Think nothing of it", Tom casually replied.

Easier said than done. That brief conversation would haunt Laura for days.

Johnnie and Hayley were sitting on a bench in the park near the Alice in Wonderland fountain. Johnnie lit up a nice, fat joint and passed it to Hayley.

"By the way, I think I found my tolerance level", Hayley informed Johnnie. "In the words of the immortal Buzz Lightyear: 'To infinity and beyond'".

"I like the way you think, Hayley Girl", Johnnie chuckled.

He leaned over and started to kiss her when they were suddenly interrupted by a familiar voice.

"Wow, I hope I'm not intruding", Brendan said, feeling a bit bolder having already broken the ice at the diner. "What a crazy coincidence", he continued, "running into you twice in one day like this, Johnnie Boy."

"Yeah, what a crazy coincidence. Why the fuck are you stalking me, Brendan?" Johnnie wanted to know. "What is it that you're up to?"

"Is that any way to talk to an old friend in front of a beautiful young woman like this?" Brendan shot back.

"We were never friends, Brendan. Circumstance threw us together, the same way it drove us apart. What's with all this 'buddy-buddy' shit now, anyway?" Johnnie asked.

"Easy, Bro. There you go again with that paranoia bullshit. Nobody's 'stalking' you, I'd just like to have the opportunity to catch up, that's all", Brendan explained. "By the way", he addressed Hayley. "I'm Brendan McAvoy, an old friend of Jr. here."

"Hayley", she replied in a very non-committal way. "Good to meet you, I think?"

"We're not friends. I thought we'd already established that", Johnnie reiterated.

"Well, that's my cue to leave – unless, of course, you'd like me to stay?" Hayley told Johnnie. "I'll be fine Hayley, thanks", Johnnie informed her.

"Looks like you two have some old scores to settle anyway. I'll see you later", she continued, giving Johnnie a quick peck on the cheek. "Brendan – not so sure it was good to meet you after all."

"Hot stuff, Johnnie", Brendan said after Hayley was gone. "You've come a long way since the freak-show act at Greenwich High."

"I'm really glad you approve, Brendan. It means so much to me", Johnnie played along. "Seriously, why the fuck are you here? You didn't run into me by accident."

"Well, for starters, I'd like a couple of hits of that joint if that's ok with you."

"Mr. Jock, looking to smoke some weed?" Johnnie said. "I'm finding that hard to believe. What made you finally break down?"

"Long story. So are you gonna share, or what?" Brendan asked.

Johnnie, allowing curiosity to get the best of him, passed Brendan the joint. "Why the fuck not? Couldn't make things any weirder than they already are."

"Let's not get into it right away, John", Brendan suggested. "Let's chat a bit first and let me get a little buzz on."

"What is it you want to 'chat' about, Brendan?" Johnnie wondered, thinking maybe he'd thought too harshly of Brendan in the past. What was it even based upon? They were just kids. He realized he didn't really know anything about Brendan.

"Nothing in particular. I mean, there's a lot to catch up on after all this time, wouldn't you think?" Brendan said, after which he took a nice long toke on that doobie.

Hayley walked into her apartment, stripped down and drew herself a hot bath. She was thinking about the strange encounter she just had with Johnnie and that weird guy, Brendan. Something wasn't quite right but she couldn't put her finger on it.

From her position lying in the tub with the bathroom door open, she could see the portrait she painted of Johnnie lying on the futon. She was suddenly aroused and wished Johnnie was there with her. In the meantime, she settled on taking care of such matters with her own two hands. At least this was something she *could* put her finger on.

Tom, freshly showered and shaved, walked out of the bathroom and went into his closet to pick out a suit. Laura happened to be in the bedroom getting dressed as well. "Boy, it sure is a lot quitter around the office without Big John screaming at everyone", Tom commented out of the blue. Laura couldn't bring herself to respond. The chasm of silence between them had grown so wide over the past few days that the sound of his voice actually startled her. "I don't know", Tom continued. "I kinda miss that miserable son-of-a-bitch. What about you, Laura dear, do you miss Big John, too? Huh! You ever wonder where he got the nickname 'Big John'? I mean he was not a particularly big guy, after all" Tom went on without giving Laura a chance to respond. "And how about *my* good fortune? Big John gets wiped off the face of the earth and I become CEO of the company. It's so strange, isn't it? You just never know what's gonna happen tomorrow. One man's loss is another man's gain, they say. Do you believe that Laura? That one man's loss is another man's gain?"

Laura, gathering her wits, managed a reply. "What's gotten into you, Tom? You're acting awfully strange. Why all the crazy questions? Are you having a mid-life crises or something?" she asked.

"A crises, perhaps; but I'm not sure it has anything to do with mid-life", Tom replied. "Did you ever wonder, Laura, why it is that people, each and every one of us, are capable of carrying out magnificent acts of kindness on the one hand, and monstrous acts of cruelty on the other? I wonder about that, Laura. I wonder about that a lot."

"I'm not following you, Tom", Laura said as she busily tried on different outfits without considering whether or not any of them looked good on her. She was on autopilot now. That's how Laura reacted to stress. As long as she kept moving, she rationalized; she'd stay ahead of the problem. "What's wrong with you? Are you having a nervous breakdown?" she wanted to know.

"Not that I'm aware of", Tom replied. "But haven't you ever stopped to think about how that could be so? I mean, most of us live somewhere in the middle, I suppose; but what is it that keeps us in check? What is it that keeps the majority of the people on the planet from acting horribly? Is it God? Is there even a God out there? I mean, who knows? Maybe the very concept of "God" is part and parcel of some evolutionary process. I'm having a hard time understanding all this, Laura. Do you have any ideas that could possibly shed some light on the subject?

"I'm going to call the doctor. I think you're having a nervous breakdown", Laura told Tom.

"Is that what it is, Laura? A nervous breakdown? Maybe so, dear. Maybe so. Do you ever stop to think about what happens when we die? Whether or not consciousness survives physical death? I think about that a lot, too. There's this fellow in the office that was diagnosed with late stage colon cancer. We talk a lot and it got me to thinking. He was telling me about how he and a friend of his used to try to travel on this thing called the 'astral plane'. She was a yoga instructor and into meditation and she said that in an altered state of consciousness, like when you're asleep and dreaming, or meditating deeply, your soul can actually leave your body and consciously travel to other dimensions and meet up with people you know, even people who have died. When he was in surgery, under heavy sedation, his friend happened to be teaching one of her meditation classes at the same time. When the class ended, one of her students came up to her and said that the entire time she was meditating, there was this guy hanging around the studio that she had never seen before. He looked to be in his early fifties, had salt and pepper hair and wore glasses, a nice enough looking guy. As soon as she stopped meditating, however, he was gone. The instructor said hold on a second and went into her house to retrieve a picture she had of her friend that she was using for some long distance Reiki healing or something like that. She came out and showed the picture to the woman and the woman started to tremble fiercely and cry. She said 'Oh my God, that's him! That's the guy that was here'. This guy, his name is James, says he has no recollection of being there, but apparently he was. His friend was sure of it. Isn't that weird? It really makes you wonder what happens when you die, whether you suddenly have access to all the secrets that existed when you were alive and unaware. Whether you suddenly know everything there is to know. That really would be something, wouldn't it, Laura?"

And with that, Tom's off-the-cuff monologue ended as abruptly as it began. Without uttering another word he turned and walked out of the room. Laura heard him start the car and drive off, unaware that this random discourse on spirituality would be the last words she would ever hear coming out of her husband's mouth.

Johnnie and Brendan sat on the bench, both quite stoned. "I've got an interesting story for you, John.

Something you'd never have imagined in your wildest dreams" Brendan informed him.

"Enough with the hype. Just tell me what the fuck is going on", Johnnie demanded.

"Ok, here goes – a couple of years ago, before your parents died, my mother sat me down for a little heart-to-heart while my father was out of the house. I couldn't imagine what she was going to tell me but I knew it couldn't be good. She was shaking and sweating and had a really hard time spitting it out. I figured she was gonna tell me she was dying or something. What she told me freaked me out even more. She told me that my father, Tom, isn't my biological father – that she had had an affair and gotten pregnant. But Tom doesn't know anything about this. She doesn't think he could handle it", Brendan said as he paused to catch his breath.

"Well, that's pretty fucked up of your mother, but what has any of this got to do with me?" Johnnie needed to understand.

"It's got everything to do with you, John. As it turns out, me and you are brothers", Brendan told him.

"Get the fuck outta here. That's insane", Johnnie insisted.

"That may be so, but it's true", Brendan continued. "The guy my mother was having the affair with, the guy she was banging behind my father's back, was Big John Reinhartsen, *your* father. *Our* father, actually, who art probably *not* in heaven. How do you feel about that, Broseph?"

At about the same time Brendan was spilling the beans to Johnnie, Tom was driving on the Taconic State Parkway, heading toward the city. It took years for him to come to terms with the secrets he'd been holding onto but now he knew what he had to do. It was all crystal clear. He could live with Laura's infidelity. He could even live with the fact that Brendan wasn't his own flesh and blood – he loved the boy just the same. But there were some secrets he just couldn't live with anymore. Some secrets are just too heavy to carry around. They wear you down, little by little. They rear their ugly heads at the most inopportune times. Secrets are bad things; they always find a way to haunt you. Laura's secrets nearly drove her insane. Tom's secrets had a better success ratio. Nothing is ever what it seems. We create our own little realities and hope that others see things the way we see them. But that's rarely ever the case.

Hayley sat on the futon in her bathrobe still thinking about Johnnie. That boy had secrets, no doubt. We all do. But she had a strong suspicion that the secrets Johnnie and Brendan were divulging to one another were not your run of the mill variety. Although she'd only known Johnnie for a few days, she felt oddly connected to him. There was something about him. He was right, she thought. She *was* falling for him. In fact, she was already in deep.

CHAPTER SIX

When Johnnie was about 10 years old, Big John took him out on the boat for a little father-son fishing trip. It was just the two of them. It was the first and only time they would do anything alone together. Johnnie wasn't sure what to expect because he knew Big John was prone to spontaneous fits of anger, having witnessed his father bullying his mother on a regular basis, so he was being extra vigilant not to set him off. But it seemed there was no setting Big John off that day. During the four hours they drifted around the eastern end of the Long Island Sound, dragging their lines, Big John was oddly quiet for the most part. He occasionally looked over and gave Johnnie a smile. Although Johnnie didn't understand what was going on, he hungrily devoured the rare bits of affection his father was dishing out that day. So much so, in fact, that he didn't even realize it when he hooked something big about an hour into the trip.

"Sink the hook, Johnnie! Looks like you landed a beauty. A striper! That's good eating, son. *Very* good eating. Look at the size of that thing!" Big John went on. "Must be 25 lbs! Let him run a little – keep the drag on but let him pull for a couple of minutes, it'll get him good and tired."

Johnnie was deliriously happy at that moment. He was unfamiliar with this side of his father's personality but he wasn't going to let that stop him from absorbing every last bit of Big John's attention. "Get the net, Daddy! He's getting close to the boat", Johnnie yelled.

"I got it, boy! Now go slow, you don't want to lose him after putting up such a magnificent fight", Big John informed his son. "Walk him around to the stern, but *slowly*, boy. I'll get the net under him and we'll show that son-of-a-bitch what this vessel looks like topside."

During the short walk back to his apartment building Johnnie remembered that moment as though it had happened only yesterday. The long-suppressed memory made him smile. It's funny, he thought; no matter how much you fucking hate someone, and no matter how solid the reason for harbouring such resentment, one small act of kindness can be all it takes for you to open up and let that person back in. The time spent on the boat alone with Big John was probably the happiest of Johnnie's young life. For those four hours he actually loved and felt love from his father. He felt close to him. "At least I have that", he thought.

On the way back to shore that afternoon, Big John's paternal instincts once again kicked into high gear. "You know, you should be careful about whom you trust and let into your life as you get older, John. Everybody has a skeleton in their closet; everyone has an axe to grind. One minute they're your best friend, the next minute they're sticking a knife in your back."

"Why would someone want to stick a knife in my back, Daddy?" Johnnie asked. "Wouldn't I die if they did that?"

"I don't mean an actual knife, son", Big John explained. "It's a figure of speech. What I mean is that most people will think nothing of causing you harm if it means protecting themselves or their families, or anything else they have an interest in. Most people are capable of doing terrible things when push comes to shove. We're not as far removed from our primal past as we would like to believe. Just remember that, John. There are only two guarantees in life once you get born: one day you will die and, in between, people will let you down. Count on no one but yourself, boy. That's the best advice I can give you. Try and remember that, will you, John?"

"I will daddy", said Johnnie, not that he had the slightest idea what his father was talking about.

"He took that better than I thought he would", Brendan said to himself as he opened the door to his hotel room. "I wonder if he'll take it as well when I lay part two on him."

Brendan hadn't spoken to his parents since arriving in the city. He decided he'd give them a quick call to let them know he was ok.

"Hi Mom. Haven't spoken to you in a few days. Just wanted to let you know I was fine", Brendan said when Laura picked up the phone.

"Oh Brendan, thank God you called – I've been trying to reach you all morning", Laura replied. "I have some terrible news, honey."

"Sorry, my battery died and I just got back to the room to plug it in", Brendan told her. "What's up?"

"Your father was driving on the Taconic this morning and lost control of his car. He went through the guardrail and down the embankment. He didn't make it, Brendan. Your father is dead", Laura explained through her sobs.

"Fuck me", was all Brendan could say when he heard the news.

"Fuck me", was all Hayley could say as Johnnie brought her up to speed on the conversation he'd just had with his "brother".

"And that's not all, Hayley. I didn't quite tell you everything. I wasn't sure it was something I wanted to share but I feel like I've known you forever and I don't feel right keeping things from you", Johnnie continued. "When we first met and I told you I was writer, you asked me what I was writing about. I told you I was writing about a kid who killed his parents for the inheritance."

"I remember, but what's that got to do with anything?" Hayley inquired.

"Well, for starters, I'm not really a writer", Johnnie fessed up.

"Holy shit, Johnnie! How could you deceive me like that?" Hayley mocked. "I don't know if I can be with you anymore. But how 'bout a quikie for the road?"

"Be serious for a minute, Hayley", Johnnie requested. "When I told you what I was 'writing' about you asked if I was influenced by those break-in murders in Greenwich a coupla years ago. Do you remember that?"

"I do, Johnnie. But please get to the point, you're starting to freak me out a little", Hayley said.

"The point is those people that got killed in Connecticut were my mother and father", Johnnie informed her.

"Holy Fuck, I'm so sorry Johnnie. That's awful. What the fuck is wrong with God?" Hayley commiserated. "He lets people do the most fucked up things."

"I suppose, but he probably did me a favor - they weren't very nice people", Johnnie offered. "I mean, maybe they were when they were younger, before I was around. But money and the stress of raising a child you probably never wanted can do fucked up things to people. In this case, it brought out the ugliness in my parents. Being wealthy was what defined them. Being good parents didn't seem to be important to them at all. My father walked around pissed off at the world even though he had everything you could ever want. He barely acknowledged my fucking existence. And my mom wasn't much better, but that's because she was drunk all the time. And I'm pretty sure she hated him. They used to fight constantly and sometimes it got physical. I remember one time when I was twelve or thirteen, they we're having a brutal argument over God knows what and he slapped her with the back of his hand, knocking her down. Maybe he'd done it before but that was the first time I'd ever witnessed it. I didn't know what to do so I ran over and jumped on him to make him stop. He reached around, grabbed me with one hand and flung me across the room like I was an old coat he couldn't stand wearing anymore. After that I just did my best to steer clear of him. "

"I don't mean to be insensitive Johnnie, but you're not gonna tell me you killed them, are you?" Hayley asked.

"I'd be lying if I said I hadn't thought about it", Johnnie said. "I'm just not the killing type, Hayley. My father had plenty of enemies, he was a pretty ruthless businessman; it could've been any one of a large number of people. All I know for sure is it wasn't me."

"And, so, that means you're not 22, either. And your name's not 'Cook'" Hayley stated, matter-of-factly.

"Correct. I'm 18. I had to wait two long years to get control of my inheritance – I was 16 when my parents were killed – and I was forced to live with my aunt and uncle, who sucked even more than my parents, during that time. As you've probably figured out by now, the inheritance didn't come from my grandfather; it came from my mother and father, John and Jacqueline Reinhartsen. So, where does that leave me and you?" Johnnie wondered.

"Where do you want it to leave us, Johnnie?" Hayley hedged.

"I'd like it to leave us right where we are", said Johnnie.

"Me, too", Hayley said with a sigh of relief. "Me, too. Life sure has a lot of crazy twists and turns", Hayley said as she and Johnnie climbed into bed. "Are you ok? I mean that was some heavy shit Brendan laid on you."

"What can I do? I mean, there is still the question of whether or not he's even telling the truth".

"Yeah, that's a good point. It didn't seem to me like he suddenly sprang this on you because he was excited to find out he had a brother after all these years", Hayley commented. "But there must be some reason why he suddenly showed up like this."

"The money, no doubt. I suppose we'll just have to wait to see", Johnnie conceded.

"You're doing a lot of 'supposing' yourself these days, Johnnie Boy", Hayley warned. "Isn't it weird how easily people rub off on each other", said Hayley. "We're all so fucking impressionable."

"Yeah, well, I wouldn't mind rubbing off on *you* before we go to sleep. Whaddaya say, Hayley Girl?" Johnnie suggested.

Johnnie was glad to have Hayley by his side. But the thought of her letting other guys 'rub off on her' was becoming a pebble in his shoe. More unfamiliar territory for Johnnie. Still, he said nothing.

Brendan went up to his room, closed the door, and opened the letter his mother had given him. It was from his father, apparently written the morning he drove off, never to return. His hands shook and tears welled in his eyes as he began to read:

Dearest Brendan,

My beautiful son. If you are reading this letter I would have to assume you've already heard the news. I want you to know how sorry I am for causing you and your mother pain. That was never my intention. What happened today was not an accident. I have been thinking about this day for a long, long time. I planned things very carefully so that no one else would be injured by my cowardly act. I hope that is the case – that no one else was injured.

Please forgive me for taking the easy way out and know that what I've done has nothing whatsoever to do with you. I loved you yesterday, I love you today and I will love you tomorrow. What happened today is the result of a very bad error in judgment on my part; a mistake made years ago that left a stain I could not scrub off, no matter how hard I tried. Please know that I did not make this decision lightly. I felt I had no other choice.

Life is funny, son. There's just no way of knowing what lies up ahead. Some of us are blessed and coast right through, while others are destined to struggle at every turn. I wish I knew what the criteria was for either / or, but unfortunately I'm not that smart. There must be some rhyme or reason to all of it. I stop short of saying that it's all the result of random activity. My educated brain tells me to believe that for every action there is a reaction, but my soul wants so badly to believe that there's more to it than that - that there is some divine force that guides us all. Whether or not that's "God"? I don't know. Again, I'm not that smart. But, if I'm lucky, I may be getting those answers right now, just as you sit and read these words I left behind.

Remember to stay true to all we've discussed while walking through the woods together over the years. Of my five-odd decades on earth, those are my fondest memories – walking through the woods and talking with you. But do not use me as an example of how you should live your life. Be kind and be guided by your conscience, by that little voice in your head that tells you when you're straying off course. You're stronger than I ever was Brendan. It's in your DNA. Take advantage of that.

And, in the future, when you think of me, smile; and know that I will be smiling over you.

With much love and affection, my son.

Dad

"It's in your DNA. He knew", Brendan thought, as tears streamed down his face. He walked over to his desk, took a book of matches out of the drawer and lit the note on fire. He watched as paper turned to ash in his waste basket. "For every action there's a reaction" he thought, as his father's words crumbled beneath him.

CHAPTER SEVEN

Johnnie awoke to the intoxicating aroma of bacon frying and coffee brewing.

"Wow, I haven't been treated to wake-up smells this good since I was a kid. My mother used to make bacon and eggs on Sunday mornings when she wasn't too hung over, which wasn't very often", Johnnie shared. "What's gotten into you this morning?"

"Nothing's gotten into me, other than you", Hayley corrected him. "And, technically, you still are a kid. I just thought it would be nice to eat in for a change."

"Sounds good to me. How'd you sleep", Johnnie asked.

"Not great, I couldn't stop thinking about Brendan. How well do you know him, anyway?" Hayley wondered.

"Why do you ask?" Johnnie wondered.

"Because if it turns out he really is your brother, he'd be entitled to half your inheritance."

"I'm well aware", Johnnie replied. "You think that's why he's here? I mean maybe he legit wants to establish some sort of relationship with me now that he thinks we're bros."

"Yeah, and they all lived happily ever after", Haley replied sarcastically. "Don't be naive, Johnnie. Of course he's here to claim his inheritance. Half of your father's estate would amount to a pretty big pile of money, I would imagine", she continued. "But I can't help thinking there's more to it than that. There's something about this guy that brings out the grassy-knoll-conspiracy-theorist in me. If we take what I admit might be one crazy leap forward, wouldn't what your father did present him with enough of a motive to commit an atrocious crime if he thought he could get away with it? Particularly if, after finding out about the affair, he felt the need to seek revenge on behalf of his real father, the one that raised him, the one that was most effected by *your* father's selfishness? That would give him even more incentive, wouldn't it? Settling a score for someone he loved *and* getting a giant payday in the process? " Hayley proposed. "Do you think Brendan's capable of something like that, Johnnie?"

"I think maybe you miscalculated your tolerance level, honey. That's some insane shit you're throwing my way", Johnnie replied.

"Maybe so, but that's how my brain works", Hayley informed him. "Think about it - it happens all the time - ordinarily sane people driven to acts of insanity for all kinds of reasons; compelled to do things they would never even consider doing under normal circumstances."

The intercom buzzed and startled Johnnie. He walked over to the house phone, wondering what was up. He wasn't expecting company.

"Hello?" Johnnie answered.

"Good morning Mr Reinhartsen, you have a visitor. Says his name is Brendan McAvoy. What would you like me to do with Mr McAvoy, sir", the doorman asked.

"Ask him what he wants, Al", Johnnie replied. After another minute or so Al replied.

"He said it's important. And private. Needs to talk to you right away", he told Johnnie.

"Send him up, I suppose", he told the doorman.

Johnnie heard his front door open and watched as Brendan walked right in and helped himself to a good look around, which instantly annoyed him. *"Jesus Christ*, nice digs", Brendan commented. "Your old man must have left you with a boatload of cash to be able to afford a crib like this. Did you buy or do you rent?" Brendan wanted to know.

"None of your fucking business, 'Broseph'", said Johnnie. "And this bit about us being 'brothers' – I'm just supposed to take your word for it? 'Cause I'd have to be a real asshole to take news like that at face value."

"I'm happy to back it up with science, Bro. Just say the word", Brendan offered. "Oh, hi Hayley. It's nice to you again. How've you been?"

"Save it Brendan, you're not fooling me", Hayley replied. "You're obviously up to something. Why don't you just man-up and tell Johnnie what it is instead of wasting his time with all the childish play-acting?"

"Not sure what you're talking about Hayley." Brendan informed her.

With that, she turned and walked into the bedroom, obviously annoyed.

"So", Johnnie uttered. "What is it this time, Brendan?"

"What it is, John, is a new fucking chapter in this nightmare of a story", Brendan answered. "Seems my dad, better known as Tom McAvoy, decided to see how well his Lexus could handle a steep embankment off the Taconic this morning. Turns out, not so well. Tom is no more. My mother is fucking crazy and I couldn't deal with her so I walked out of the house with just enough money in my pocket for a train ticket to the city and came straight here. Had nowhere else to go, Johnnie. I'm broke, I'm homeless, and I'm hungry to boot. Any chance you could put a 'brother' up for a few days while he tries to figure out what comes next?" Brendan asked.

"I haven't seen you in years and now you want to move in?" Johnnie said, exasperated. "Why the fuck would I agree to that?"

"Because it's the right thing to do?" Brendan suggested.

"Are you serious? About Tom, I mean?" Johnnie asked.

"Afraid so", Brendan answered. "Pretty fucked up, huh?"

"Very fucked up. I always liked Tom", Johnnie offered. "He was a really good guy, always nice to me. Why would he do something like that?"

"Don't know for sure but he left a note, addressed to me. Said he was carrying around some horrible secret he could no longer live with. Something he was involved with years ago but he didn't mention what it was. Sounds mysterious, huh?" Brendan said.

"Very. Well, under the circumstances, I'd be a real dick to turn you away", Johnnie said. "So, even though it's against my better judgement, you can have the extra bedroom for a couple of days. I think there's some left-over Chinese food in the fridge if you're hungry. But whatever you do, do not fucking antagonize Hayley. We've got a pretty nice thing working and I don't need you to fuck it up for me."

"I'll do my best", Brendan promised. "But back to the mysterious circumstances surrounding my father's suicide – I've been racking my brains trying to figure out what his secret could be; what he could have done that was so unforgivable he felt he had no choice but to kill himself? The only thing that even remotely makes sense is that it has something to do with Big John and Jacquie. I mean, do you think it's possible he was somehow involved in what happened to them? Could that be the horrible secret he's been carrying around?"

"Anything's possible. Did he know about Big John and your mom?" Johnnie asked.

"He knew, for sure", Brendan said. "Jesus, how much more insane can things get?"

"I don't know that there's a limit", Johnnie replied. "It's like a fucking video game. As soon as you get to the end of one level of insanity, you get thrust into the next.

It's a fucking endless cycle. I'm sorry about Tom, that really sucks."

"Yeah, well; thanks for putting me up, and for putting up with me. I know you and I were never really close, John; and this is all pretty weird, but I just can't hang out with my mother right now. She's on this trip where everything has to be about her", Brendan told Johnnie. "She's the one that told me about her and Big John to begin with. And she did it just to get it off her chest and make herself feel better. She didn't give a fuck about how it would affect me. Gonna take me a while to get over that", Brendan continued.

"Yeah, well about Big John and your mother", Johnnie said. "It wouldn't be a bad idea for both of us to get DNA tested to confirm the story. At least we can be sure one way or another. I know there's a place on West 49th street that does genetic testing. My father's sister brought me there after my parents died and she took me in. She wanted to make sure I was actually Big John's son", Johnnie continued. "She was hoping I wasn't so she'd get the inheritance, fucking cunt. They probably still have all my records so hopefully it will be quick."

"Anytime you want to go. Tomorrow is fine by me", Brendan said.

"Cool, let's just do it then and get it out of the way. But if you're fucking with me Brendan, tell me now. I don't feel like having my time wasted if you already know what the answer is, and I don't want to have to kick the shit out of you on top of it", Johnnie warned.

"Listen to you, all rough and tumble and shit! I'm not fucking with you", Brendan promised. "You know what I know. If anyone's lying it's my mother. I guess we'll find out tomorrow."

"I guess so", Johnnie said.

Brendan walked into the kitchen while Johnnie walked into the bedroom to see how Hayley was doing and bring her up to speed on current events. She didn't look happy when he walked in. "I've already heard", she informed Johnnie. "These walls aren't as soundproof as they're advertised to be."

"So, you know that I've agreed to let Brendan crash here for a few days 'til he figures out his next move. He's got to go back to Connecticut for his father's funeral by the end of the week anyway", Johnnie let her know.

"It's your house, Johnnie", she reminded him. "You can do whatever you want. But, if you want my opinion, I wouldn't trust Brendan as far as I could throw him until I found out what he was really after."

"Maybe he legit wants to establish some sort of relationship with me", Johnnie shot back. "He's agreed to go for genetic testing tomorrow to clear up any doubts. We'll take it from there. Besides, there's something kinda cool about the idea of having a brother."

"Are you fucking kidding me?" Hayley replied. "This guy shows up out of nowhere claiming to be your closest living relative, and you think there's something 'kinda cool' about it? Johnnie, you've got a lot at stake here. He's fucking scamming you because he wants your money."

"That's why we're doing the test – to see if this is for real", Johnnie answered, a little less patiently now.

"So, how and when did his father die, anyway?" Hayley wanted to know.

"He committed suicide this morning. Drove his car off a cliff on the Taconic. He left a note for Brendan saying he could no longer live with some horrible secret he had, but didn't say what it was", Johnnie told her. "Brendan was wondering if it could have had something to do with my mother and father's murders, if that's what his horrible secret was. Doesn't seem all that far-fetched, actually."

"It could also be that Brendan himself was involved. Maybe he knew about his mother and your father before his mother ever even told him about it and put two and two together regarding the inheritance. It would be easy enough for him to put it on his father now that he's dead and there are no longer any consequences", Hayley posed. "That's not so far-fetched either."

"Oh, so we're back to that theory– that Brendan killed my parents to inherit half the estate?" Johnnie responded, condescendingly. He was confused. He didn't understand why he was suddenly caught somewhere between being with Hayley and having a brother. Both relationships appeared out of the blue within weeks of each other and both were equally genuine as far as he was concerned. So why did he feel like he was he being forced to make a choice? Why couldn't he have both? True, he didn't know Brendan very well but if it turned out they were blood brothers it would change everything.

Hayley, on the other hand, liked the way things were coming together for her and Johnnie. The last thing she needed was for this clown Brendan to step into the middle of it and fuck things up for her. She wanted Brendan out of the picture. If she could just get Johnnie to believe her theory it would go a long way toward getting the job done.

Johnnie and Brendan walked into Empire Genetics early the next morning.

"What is it you're looking to establish, Mr Reinhartsen?" the technician asked.

"We're looking to confirm whether or not Brendan here is my biological half-brother. If we share the same paternal bloodline", Johnnie explained.

"Well, that's easy enough. We'll just need to swipe some saliva from the inside of his cheek. It'll take about an hour to get the results", the technician informed them. "You came at a good time; the sperm is slow today - Ha! Forgive me. It's an old geneticist's joke."

As Johnnie and Brendan sat waiting for their life-altering test results to emerge they chatted about Tom, Big John and Jacquie, and the absurd situation they'd been sucked into through no fault of their own. It seems that their old friend - circumstance - had come full circle, uniting the two once again. For better or worse, they might finally have something substantial in common.

"Dude, who'd of thought the two of us would be sitting here one day waiting to find out if we were fucking *brothers*?" Brendan half asked, half blurted.

"In a million fucking years I never would have considered it", Johnnie replied. "You were pretty much a douchebag to me when we were kids. If it turns out we're blood we might have to re-think the relationship."

"A lot has changed since we were kids, bro. We should probably re-think the relationship regardless", Brendan suggested.

"I suppose", Johnnie replied but he didn't seem all that convinced.

The technician returned exactly 60 minutes later with the lab results. Johnnie and Brendan held their breath as they waited for him to speak. "Congratulations", the technician said. "It's a boy. *Two* boys, actually. There's no doubt about it, you two are siblings. Is there anything else I can do for you?"

"No, that's more than enough for one day", Johnnie informed him.

Hayley was getting ready for work when Johnnie returned later that evening. She looked ridiculously hot, he thought, a prerequisite for her chosen profession. But as he stood in the doorway watching her carefully arrange the final bow on a package that would make any man shudder; the only thing he felt was the knot in his stomach pulling tighter.

"Oh, hey", she said with a smile. "How long you been standing there?"

"Long enough", he told her.

"You still like what you see, Johnnie Boy?" Haley asked.

"More than you know, Girl. More than you know", he replied with a hint of sadness in his voice.

"So, what did you find out this afternoon?" Haley wondered.

"I found out I have a brother", Johnnie told her.

"Really! A real, live brother! And how do you feel about that? I mean, it's a pretty big deal, right?" Hayley offered, somewhat facetiously.

"Yeah, it's a *very* big deal. And you know what? I feel kinda pumped about it", Johnnie answered. "I know that sounds weird but it's the truth. You come from a big family so I don't expect you to understand, but after having been an only child my entire life, and then an orphan to boot; it feels pretty good to suddenly have a brother."

"Well, I'm glad you're happy but I have to tell you, I still think something's not right with this picture. You could be in danger, Johnnie. I mean, what if he *was* somehow involved in your parent's deaths? What's to stop him from finishing the job and collecting the entire inheritance, which he would now be entitled to because you've just established the connection?" Hayley replied.

As much as Johnnie hated to admit it, what Hayley was saying made sense. But he wasn't yet ready to give up the buzz he'd been enjoying all day. If Brendan did kill Big John and Jacquie, he wouldn't feel all that differently he supposed. After all, Big John had completely fucked up the guy's life. He could see how Brendan could be driven to extremes under such circumstances. And the truth was Johnnie didn't really care that they were gone. Being an orphan didn't faze him in the least. But the business about the inheritance didn't make sense. Tom made plenty of money and was always very generous with Brendan. That part just didn't add up. It's amazing how easily we can rationalize and overlook things if we want something badly enough, Johnnie thought. He decided to change the subject.

"Why don't you blow off work tonight and you and I can go out, have a nice dinner and then watch a movie or something later", Johnnie suggested.

"Well, as nice as that all sounds, I've got to go make some money. I mean, I'm not exactly killing it as an artist", Hayley reminded him. "If I don't work, who's gonna pay my bills?" Hayley asked innocently enough.

"I am", Johnnie shot back without the slightest hesitation. "And while you're at it, why don't you just move in with me? I'll continue to pay your rent and we can fix up your place as a proper art studio. Then you won't have to let sleazy motherfuckers rub all over you while their buddies drool and you pretend to enjoy it", Johnnie argued. "Whaddaya say?"

"I say that's a very intriguing offer, and I'm flattered that you want to take care of me; but I don't know", Hayley replied. "I don't like to depend on anyone but myself. In my experience, you allow yourself to become dependent on other people and the next thing you know, they're not there anymore."

"That's funny, that's the one piece of advice my father ever gave me – count on no one but yourself. That doesn't seem like a very healthy way to live though", Johnnie told Hayley. "But you don't have to worry; I *want* to take care of you. I've got more money than I know what to do with. No strings attached. If things don't work out, I'll fund you until you get back on your feet. That's a promise. Come on Hayley – I couldn't possibly make things any easier for you."

"Let me think about it, Johnnie", Hayley replied. "It's a very sweet offer, it's just that it's a big decision for me to make."

"Ok. I don't mean to pressure you. I just feel like you shouldn't have to give lap dances to scuzzballs to make ends meet. It's beneath you", Johnnie said, calling an end to the conversation.

Johnnie and Brendan tore silently into the Chinese food that had just arrived. Johnnie was first to speak. "So, how do you feel about having a brother after being an only child your whole life?" he asked Brendan.

"You want me to answer that honestly?" Brendan said.

"Well there's no point in answering if you're not going to be honest about it", Johnnie lectured. "Enough with the secrets and the lies and all the other bullshit our parents forced us to live with our whole lives. We've just been given an opportunity to set the record straight. We should take advantage of it. I don't know about you but I, for one, don't want to end up like the miserable fucks they turned into because we can't be straight with each other."

"That makes two of us, Bro", Brendan agreed. "You know, when we were younger you and I spent a lot of time around each other but, like you said, we never really became friends. We never really even got to know each other. I used to think you were a freak. I still think you were a freak, but I'm talking past tense. Since your parents died you've become a whole different person. You've really pulled your shit together. You no longer act like a weirdo; you've even got a hot girlfriend. You've become *normal*, or as close to normal as anyone who smokes as much weed as you can be, I suppose. That was meant as a compliment, just in case you didn't catch it. Truth is, I'm liking the idea of having you as a brother."

"Yeah, I picked up on the compliment. So generous of you", Johnnie joked. "I mean, I didn't like you very much when we were growing up, either. Everything always came so easily for you: you were a big-time athlete, an A student, you had a million friends, girls were all over you; and you even got along with your parents. I had none of that so I just kind of checked out. I guess I never really knew you. But I'm cool with having you as a brother."

"I did have it pretty easy when we were kids", Brendan went on. "But all that changed a couple of years ago when my mom told me about her and your asshole father. I have to say I was so pissed off when she told me all I could do from that point on was plot how I was going to get even with that motherfucker for wrecking my life. I lost all respect for my mother; and I couldn't even look at Tom anymore. Everything was suddenly foreign to me. Then I heard about the murders and I thought well, at least that takes care of one of my problems. But I still didn't feel like the score was settled. Then it dawned on me that if Big John was my father, that meant you and I were brothers. I don't know why I never caught on earlier. And if you and I were brothers that meant I was entitled to half of Big John's estate. My plan was to find you and demand my share, just to fuck with you more than anything. I didn't need the money – Tom provided for us pretty well. I just wanted to cause you pain. But all that has changed over the past few days. It's funny, we have these preconceived notions about people and the way things are, but in the end we really don't know shit about anything. Nothing is ever black and white. Everything is grey."

"I get it, and I'm even cool with you getting your share of the pie given the circumstances; there's more than enough to go around", Johnnie told Brendan, surprising himself as the words left his mouth. "But as long as we're walking down the path of brutal honesty, I have to say; after what you've just told me, it would be pretty fucking easy for someone to point to you as a prime suspect in the murders. I mean, you had the motive and the incentive to go to extremes, you just said so yourself: You knew about Big John and Laura prior to the murders; you were furious with him for betraying Tom and turning your life upside down; and you stood to inherit a fortune if Big John and Jacquie were out of the picture. Like I said, it wouldn't be a stretch to implicate you once you have all that background info. I'd be careful who I shared that shit with if I were you."

"Do you think I killed Big John and Jacquie?" Brendan asked straight up.

"No, I really don't", Johnnie replied honestly. "But whomever did is still out there and the police have no idea where. I never did buy into that 'home invasion' bullshit. There's just no way it was a random act of violence. Big John was ruthless and had lots of enemies. Any one of a hundred people could have done it. It was probably someone he fucked hard who couldn't wait to get even. Our father thought he was untouchable and treated everyone like shit. No surprise at the way things turned out for him."

When all but the wilted lettuce from the bottom of the General Tsao's Chicken container had been consumed, Johnnie and Brendan retired to the living room where they sat down on the couch and lit up a joint. It had been a long day, one that the two would likely not forget anytime soon. This was going to take some getting used to. But Johnnie and Brendan appeared as though they were off to a good start, all things considered.

"I'm fucking stuffed", Brendan told Johnnie. "You feel like going out for a while, I need a distraction."

"Hayley's working tonight", Johnnie said. "So I wouldn't mind doing something."

"Where's she working?" Brendan asked. The two were being uncharacteristically civil as they attempted to get a feel for how brothers were supposed to act toward each other.

"She works at a club in midtown", Johnnie told him.

"Waitressing?"

"Stripping."

"You're *shitting* me", Brendan responded.

"I shit you not", Johnnie corrected him. "And I'm not liking it. When we first met she mentioned that that's how she made her living but I really didn't think twice about it, other than the fleeting fantasy that I might get to bang a stripper. But a few days later I realized I was very much into hanging with her and the idea of her humping sleezeballs all night became a problem for me."

"Are you gonna do anything about it?" Brendan wondered.

"Not sure there's anything I *can* do", Johnnie answered. "Before you got back tonight I asked her to blow off work and hang with me but she said she couldn't. She needed to make money to pay her bills."

"What did you say?" asked Brendan.

"I told her *I'd* pay her bills. And I told her she should move in with me. That she could keep the apartment downstairs and we'd turn it into a real studio for her to paint in", Johnnie said.

"So when's she moving in?" Brendan wanted to know.

"I don't know that she is", Johnnie answered. "She's got this thing about remaining independent –she won't let herself rely on someone else because she can't handle the inevitable let-down. I think it has something to do with her father. He was a fireman who died in a fire when she was little."

"No offense, brother; but is she out of her fucking mind?" Brendan replied. "Who wouldn't jump all over an offer like that?"

"Hayley, for one. That's part of what attracts me to her – her independence", Johnnie noted.

The club was more crowded than usual for a Wednesday night and Hayley found herself in constant motion, sliding from one lap to the next. As she pretended to be in love with the owner of the lap she was currently entertaining she thought about the conversation she'd had earlier with Johnnie. At that moment, she couldn't imagine a better offer. He was right – this was beneath her. But she was still having a hard time coming to terms with the idea of being "taken care of". She swore that she would never again put herself in that position. But things change. Feelings change. People change. Maybe this *could* be a good thing if she were careful about it. Then she started thinking about Brendan. It bothered her that he was going to be staying with Johnnie but she knew she had no say in the matter. She wanted him out of the picture. If she were going to move in with Johnnie she didn't need Brendan hanging around. But it didn't look like he'd be leaving anytime soon of his own accord. She needed to do something to help grease the wheels.

Johnnie and Brendan wandered out that evening with no particular destination in mind. All Johnnie knew was he felt like getting out of the neighbourhood. So the two headed downtown and wound up roaming around Tribeca, looking for someplace interesting to hang out. As they turned the corner onto Murray Street, Brendan spotted the strip club marquee. "Here we go, Johnnie Boy", Brendan sing-songed. "Just what the doctor ordered. This will take your mind off Hayley for a while."

"I don't know if I'm into it. I don't really need to have a visual of what Hayley's doing right now", Johnnie told Brendan.

"You're over thinking this, Bro", Brendan explained. "It's a well-known fact that the magical vagina dance temporarily expunges any thoughts or memories you have of your girlfriend. It's like vaginal amnesia, otherwise known as 'vagnesia'. Works like a charm. So, we going in, or what?"

"Yeah, what the fuck. I'm curious to see how well this vagnesia thing works", Johnnie agreed.

Johnnie paid the cover for both of them and they headed in. There were half a dozen dancers up on stage and countless hotties down below working the crowd, expertly assessing who the biggest schmuck in the house was. The brothers took a seat in the back and admired the talent.

"See what I mean, Bro? You're already starting to forget and no one's even touched you yet", Brendan advised. "Pure fucking magic."

"Damn! This shit is for real", Johnnie happily intoned. "We should put our affluence to good use and figure out how to bottle it up. Not only would we make a ton of money, we'd also be providing an incredibly righteous service for mankind at the same time."

"Speaking of affluence, I'm a little on the light side for the time being", Brendan said. "Can you cover me this evening?"

"It's your money too, dude. I just happen to be the one holding it", Johnnie advised. "I'll get in touch with the lawyer and accountant that settled the whole estate thing for me tomorrow and get things straightened out. Here's a few hundo to get you through the night."

"Bless you, my brother", Brendan replied. "Bless you."

"Do you have *any* idea how much your life is about to change as a result of my incredible generosity?" Johnnie asked.

"Can't say as I do, but I'm hoping it takes me in a very different direction then that last round of changes took me", Brendan replied.

Johnnie sat there, smiling. All of a sudden things were starting to make sense. He accepted that Brendan was his brother and all that other shit he'd been living with – the lies, the loneliness, the anger and the deceit - was starting to appear smaller and smaller in his rear view memory. He was thinking what he was feeling must be that thing they call "contentment". He was thinking it felt good. Then he spotted her.

Hayley was two or three dances into it with an overweight, slimy-looking businessman who was sweating and panting profusely. And she was working him like a champ. If she were allowed to ask, she'd have had his ATM card and PIN number in an instant. Not that it mattered – she was gonna get the cash out of him one way or another. It was only a matter of time.

Johnnie wasn't sure at first if his eyes were playing tricks on him, then, as he watched, he observed the signature move he'd come to know so well – her head rolling in perfect sync to her hip gyrations – and he knew immediately that the night was not going to end well.

"JesusFuckingChrist", Johnnie moaned.

"What's up, John?" Brendan asked, mildly concerned.

"Un-fucking believable", Johnnie went on. "Take a look across the room. Two O'clock. See the girl dancing on the fat-guys lap?"

"Yeah, what about her?" Brendan wanted to know.

"Keep looking", instructed Johnnie.

"Yeah, she's pretty hot, but they all are. Why are you fixated on……….Oh my fucking God!!! Are you kidding me?!" Brendan wanted to know.

"What the fuck is she doing *here*?" Johnnie asked out loud, but he was really talking to himself. "She's supposed to be working in midtown. What the fuck is she doing in Tribeca?" Johnnie went on. "This is incredibly fucked up."

"Easy, Bro", Brendan advised. "The last thing you want to do is create a scene in a place like this."

But Johnnie didn't hear a word of what his brother had just said. As he got up, Brendan grabbed him by the arm but Johnnie just flung him aside. "Fucker must be working out", Brendan thought as he did his best to keep Johnnie in check. But Johnnie was on a mission. Two of the bouncers on the other side of the room noticed immediately that something was about to go down but they were too far away to do anything about it. Johnnie acted swiftly and harshly. He picked up a half empty bottle of Carona from a table as he was about three strides away and quickly cracked it across the big man's face, cutting him badly and knocking him out. Hayley jumped back and screamed, but Brendan was on Johnnie in an instant, pulling him quickly across the floor and out the front door. But not before Hayley got a good look at the both of them. Inside the cab Brendan was screaming that Johnnie was a fucking idiot, that he could have gotten them both killed; but all Johnnie could hear were his father's words, playing over and over again in his head: "we're not as far removed from our primal past as we'd like to believe." So true, Johnnie thought. So true.

CHAPTER EIGHT

When Brendan was seven years old, right around the time one's memory really starts to stick, Tom used to take him into the city on Saturday mornings for little father-son day trips. Sometimes they'd spend the afternoon at the Central Park zoo, sometimes they'd sit by the lake, and sometimes they'd go up to Tom's office – something Brendan loved to do. "Come on, Bren; time for us men to clear out so your mom can get some time to herself. Go to the beauty parlor, do a little shopping, whatever meets her fancy", Tom would tell his son.

As Brendan lay in bed remembering those moments with a heavy heart, he also started to remember something else, something he hadn't thought about for years. He could still see his father standing under a tree near the swings, where Brendan was trying desperately to rap himself around the bar high above. But Tom was never alone. It seems he kept running into the same woman, over and over again. No matter where they went, she would suddenly appear. He remembered she was tall and pretty in an odd sort of way, with long, blonde hair. And she always wore a short skirt. Who was she? He doesn't remember seeing her anywhere other than wherever he and Tom went on those Saturday morning excursions. Then one day, she wasn't there anymore. She'd stopped appearing out of the blue. Brendan remembered the name he'd given her – "the Magic Lady" – because she appeared and disappeared without warning, the same way the lady on TV would disappear inside of a box and then show up a little while later sitting in the audience.

Whoever this woman was, Brendan remembers his father smiling non-stop whenever she was around. But after she'd stopped showing up for a while, Tom stopped taking Brendan to the city for their father-son day trips. After that, he never seemed to smile as much anymore.

Hayley got to Johnnie's apartment at 4:45 a.m. and walked straight into the bedroom. Johnnie was only half asleep, the result of the anxiety he was experiencing. He knew he would have to deal with the consequences of his actions at some point during those early morning hours. He hoped the big man wasn't hurt too bad; it's not like he was trying to disrespect anyone. He was just in the wrong place at the wrong time, same as Johnnie. Circumstance rears its ugly head once again.

Much to his surprise, Hayley stripped down and crawled into bed with him. He was waiting for the axe to fall, but instead what he got was a warm, wet kiss on the mouth. "Wow, wasn't expecting that at all", Johnnie told Hayley. "Why would you be in such a loving mood after what I did tonight? I know it was stupid, I just couldn't stop myself", Johnnie confessed. "Seeing you on top of that disgusting motherfucker sent me into a rage."

"Well, you won't have to worry about that ever happening again. I just got fired. They waited until I finished my shift to tell me", Hayley replied. "You got your wish, Johnnie Boy. Looks like I'm moving in after all."

"Seriously? That's great. I should crack people with beer bottles more often", Johnnie said, only half jokingly.

"What were you doing at the club last night anyway?" Hayley asked. "How did you even know I was going to be there?"

"I had no idea you were going to be there, you told me you were working in midtown. Brendan and I felt like getting out of the neighborhood and just happened to end up in Tribeca", Johnnie answered. "When we got to Murray Street, Brendan spotted the club and talked me into going in. I knew it was a bad idea. Worked out pretty well in the end though."

"Don't get carried away, Johnnie. I'm not exactly thrilled you put me in this position where I now have no choice but to move in", Hayley said.

"I know, and I'm sorry", Johnnie replied. "But it's all gonna work out fine. Trust me."

Johnnie set up a meeting with his lawyer from the firm of Goodwin Proctor for himself and Brendan for later that afternoon. Of course, you don't just pick up the phone and say I'm coming in at 2:00 pm when you're dealing with a high-powered New York law firm, but after Johnnie explained the full extent of the business they would be discussing, Simon Solecki, one of the firm's Senior Managing Partners, made himself readily available to meet that day.

Within a few hours Solecki, after consulting with the accountant, had set up a private banking account for Brendan at JP Morgan Chase, the same bank that held Johnnie's accounts, and arranged to have exactly one half of Johnnie's assets electronically transferred to Brendan's account within five business days. Brendan was ecstatic. After all, fifty percent of an extraordinary amount of money is an extraordinary amount of money.

"Seeing as I can no longer live with my mother after everything that's gone down I was thinking it might not be a bad idea for me to buy myself an apartment in the city", Brendan mentioned to his brother as they left their lawyers office. "I noticed there was one available in your building. Would you be opposed to me looking at it?" he wanted to know.

"Not at all bro", Johnnie replied. "In fact it would be a smart investment. To quote my real estate broker: 'real estate on Central Park West overlooking the reservoir does *not* go down in value – *ever!*' But be prepared to expose your life story to the fucking co-op board. They exist solely to cause prospective purchasers as much grief as possible. You'll want to smack them after about twenty minutes, but my advice would be to refrain from doing so if you really want to live there."

"Got it. I'll try and do a better job taking your advice then you did taking mine last night", Brendan replied.

"Can't argue with that", Johnnie said. "But fuck you anyway."

Laura chose to have a small, private service for Tom rather than a chaotic wake with everyone they knew showing up to offer condolences. She just didn't have the stomach for that. The service took place in a century old, non-denominational chapel in Darien. Only Tom's closest family and friends were invited to attend.

Brendan managed to arrive at the chapel a few minutes before the service began. Given all the distractions he'd encountered during the past week in New York City it's no wonder he was completely unprepared to see his father lying in a box without a trace of life left in him. He was even less prepared to say goodbye, knowing it would be the last time he would ever do so. The reality of Tom's passing was finally starting to sink in. Brendan was feeling the weight of the loss for the first time since Laura broke the news. He went straight over and gave his mother a long hug. He did his best to provide whatever comfort he could under the circumstances but the hug was intended more to comfort himself than anyone else, especially Laura. She immediately broke down and sobbed in his arms. "Oh, Bren. How could this have happened to me?" she cried.

"*Us*, mom", Brendan corrected her with an almost apathetic acceptance that this was the way things were going to be from now on. "It happened to *us*."

"Well, thank God you'll still be here", Laura exclaimed. "You *will* be here, won't you Bren?"

"From time to time, mom. I'm moving into an apartment in the city, but I'll visit often enough", he informed his mother.

"You can't leave me alone! What if I won't pay your rent? What about Georgetown? How will you survive? How will *I* survive if you go?" Laura asked.

"I've got all that covered, Laura", Brendan explained. "You and I have a lot to talk about, but this isn't the time or place. I'll come by the house tomorrow."

Brendan suddenly felt as though he were all grown up. He felt secure in knowing that he'd be the one calling the shots as they related to his own life from that point on. "Your world falls apart and your world comes back together again", Brendan thought to himself, remembering the words his father shared with him so long ago during their walks through the woods. "It's an endless cycle, Bren", he could hear Tom saying. "Nothing lasts forever. Your world falls apart and your world comes back together again. Its how you manage the transition that matters."

"I bet dad would be proud of the way I'm handling things", Brendan thought.

At the cemetery a small crowd gathered to pay their final respects as Tom was being laid to rest. Brendan and

Laura stood near the coffin in bewildered silence as the priest prayed to God to grant Thomas James McAvoy everlasting peace and eternal happiness alongside Him in the Kingdom of Heaven. "Please", Brendan thought to himself. "He never let the poor guy enjoy his life while he was on earth. Why the fuck would he let him enjoy it now?"

As Brendan stood there lost in his thoughts, he suddenly noticed a tall woman standing at the back of the crowd. He recognized her immediately, as if only minutes had passed since their last encounter. It was the Magic Lady, he was sure of it.

When the ceremony ended and the well wishers took turns passing along ineffectual words of wisdom to Laura, Brendan made his way to the back of the crowd. He stood behind her for a moment, unsure of what to say. As she turned to face him the words jumped out of his mouth involuntarily: "the Magic Lady", Brendan uttered.

"Excuse me?" the woman replied, as if awakened from a trance. "Do I know you?"

"You're the Magic Lady", Brendan told her again.

"I'm afraid I don't understand what that means", she said. And then she recognized him. It was the look in his eyes. She remembered the way he used to look at her as a child; it was the same way he was looking at her now. "You're Brendan, aren't you?" the Magic Lady asked.

"Why did you come here today? Did my mother invite you?" Brendan wanted to know, once again feeling very much like the seven year old child Tom used to bring to the park.

"No. I was a friend of your father's many years ago. I read about his unfortunate passing in the paper and came to pay my respects. And to say goodbye", she said.

"You were always there, every time my father and I went to the city. You would appear out of nowhere", Brendan told her. "And then you just stopped coming. How did you know my father?"

"We'd met during the course of business and became friends", she explained to Brendan.

"Why did you stop coming?" Brendan asked. "My father was the happiest I'd ever seen him whenever you were around."

"That's nice of you to say", she replied with a shy smile.

"But then you stopped showing up and he never seemed as happy", Brendan continued. "Why did you stop coming? You were more than just friends, weren't you?"

"Your dad and I, well; it's complicated, Brendan", she said.

"It all makes sense now", Brendan went on. "He was in love with you, wasn't he?"

"Your dad loved your mother very much, Brendan. Too much, maybe", she advised. "I'm afraid I have to leave now. Take good care of yourself. You've grown into a fine young man. I'm sure your father was very proud of you."

And with that, the Magic Lady disappeared for one last time.

Brendan stood there for a moment, taking it all in. The pieces were starting to fall into place. "Jesus Christ", he thought. "Is anything ever what it fucking appears to be?"

It was late when Brendan got back to his brother's apartment. He'd stopped into a couple of pubs along the way and managed to consume several beers and many shots of tequila in a foolhardy attempt to numb both his pain and his brain. Johnnie was sitting on the couch watching a movie and Hayley was already asleep. The aroma of high-end reefer permeated the room. Brendan wanted some.

"How you doing, Bro?" Johnnie inquired.

"What a fucked up day", Brendan told him. "Seeing Tom lying in a coffin really threw me. I guess up until that point I didn't believe it was real. It just seemed like I was having a bad dream. Then they lowered him into the ground. I watched as they covered him with dirt and thought about how claustrophobic he was. I imagined him waking up in that box and totally freaking. That image is gonna haunt me for the rest of my days. When my time comes, if you're still around, you need to promise you'll arrange to have me cremated. The mere *thought* of being buried in a box is enough to make me totally lose my shit."

"I'm on it, Brendan. No worries", Johnnie promised.

"Dude, you've come a long way since we were kids", Brendan noticed. "You're all hip now. New look, new cloths, new language. I gotta say, it's working for you."

"Thanks Brendan. That means a lot to me coming from you – NOT", Johnnie joked. "But seriously, are you handling this shit ok? I mean, for me it was different. I never really liked Big John and Jacquie. I mean I loved them, I guess, but it was impossible to like them. They were so fucked up in so many ways. Somehow I managed to survive the ordeal and turn out semi-normal. I guess a negative and a negative really does equal a positive. But I know you were always close to Tom and Laura."

"I was, but all that's changed now. Tom's dead and Laura betrayed him, which is probably why he's gone. It's hard for me to look at her the same way anymore. What she did was so fucked up. Maybe one day I'll be able to forgive her for it but I'd need the Hubble telescope to see it right now. It's too far away to even consider."

"I get it, but it's gonna eat you up inside. You gotta let it go", Johnnie lectured. "There are two sides to every fucked up story. It's cliché but it's true. You don't know what drove Laura to do what she did. Maybe she wasn't getting the attention she needed. Maybe Tom drove her to it. But common sense dictates that she's not gonna be able to pull it together without you. Next thing you know Laura will be the one driving the car off the cliff. Better figure it out quick or you'll be attending another funeral soon. Then you'll be an orphan, just like me."

"So, check this out", Brendan uttered. "When I was little, Tom used to take me to the city every Saturday morning without fail. We'd usually hang out in Central Park for a few hours so my mother could have some "alone time" as Tom called it. But that never really made sense to me because she had plenty of time to herself every day while I was at school and my father was at work. But I didn't care. I loved going to the city which, for me, was like going to a foreign country. And every time we went this woman would show up out of nowhere and they would both act like it was some big coincidence. I don't remember thinking anything of it at the time, and over the years I'd completely forgotten about it. Then, the other night, I was thinking about Tom and those trips to the city and all of a sudden she popped into my head. That's when I began realizing it was impossible that no matter where we were this woman would show up by sheer chance. And Tom was always so happy whenever she was around. But eventually, she stopped showing up. Fast forward to the funeral today. I was trancing out when I looked up and spotted a familiar face at the back of the crowd. It took a minute to figure it out but it was her, the Magic Lady."

"The 'Magic Lady'?" Johnnie wondered. "Where the fuck did you come up with that?"

"What difference does it make, I was like seven", Brendan chimed in. "The point is there must have been some reason why after all these years she just popped up again, out of the blue. My mother didn't invite her; she said she'd read about it in the paper and wanted to say goodbye to Tom. You get what I'm saying?" Brendan asked.

"Yeah, an old friend of your father's came to his funeral to say goodbye", Johnnie replied. "What the fuck is so unusual about that?"

"Jesus Christ, it's impossible to get through to you when you're this stoned" Brendan said. "Think about it, John. Years ago this woman would show up out of nowhere, spend an hour or two flirting with my father while I played on the swings or dug up worms or did whatever the fuck else I might have been doing, and then she'd just leave. Tom never once introduced me to her. Why wouldn't he have introduced me to her? Because he had something to hide, that's why. And when she stopped showing up, Tom stopped taking me to the city on Saturday mornings. Now do you get what I'm saying?"

"Rather than telling elaborate stories to get your point across, why don't you just tell me what you mean?" Johnnie begged. "I'm way too stoned right now to piece this mystery together."

"You're an idiot! Tom was having an affair with this woman! He knew about Laura and Big John and he went out and got even. What he probably didn't expect was that he'd fall in love in the process. Tom was as Irish Catholic as it got. Bible, Church, God, the Ten Commandments. He couldn't live with the fact that he betrayed my mother at such a deep level. It *was* what he did that eventually did him in, but it didn't have anything to do with killing Big John and Jacquie. That affair was the stain he was referring to in the note he left. Now it all makes sense. *That* was the 'error in judgement' he was talking about."

"Oh, now I get it. Why couldn't you just say that to begin with", Johnnie wanted to know. "Dude, you're not responsible for your parents mistakes", he reminded him. "They made some bad decisions, just like everyone else on the fucking planet. *They* made their bed. That doesn't mean *you* have to sleep in it, too. You can't count on other people, Bro; you can only count on yourself. Once you get born there are only two guarantees in life: one day you will die; and, in between, people will let you down. You know who told me that?"

"Some cynical fuck, no doubt", Brendan replied.

"You're absolutely right. And his name was Big John Reinhartsen", Johnnie said. "It's the only piece of advice 'dad' ever gave me, and it's starting to feel like the motherfucker knew what he was talking about."

CHAPTER NINE

"So you're now worth half of what you were worth 24 hours ago", Hayley reminded Johnnie. "How much *is* half of what you were worth yesterday, anyway?"

"More than I'll ever need Hayley, that's how much", Johnnie replied, cutting her off.

"So Brendan just waltzes into your life, pockets a gazillion fucking dollars, and you're fine with that?" Hayley wanted to know.

"He's my fucking brother, Hayley. He's entitled to the money just as much as I am", Johnnie reminded her back. "If more people did what was right instead of just doing what was right for *them*, I mean, fuck; I don't get why you have such an issue with this."

"He's your *half* brother Johnnie, and I have an issue with it because I care about you", Hayley shot back. "And I care that Brendan is taking advantage of you and you're letting him. And I care that he's inserted himself into your life and, through association, my life too. I don't trust him. You know that."

"Don't give me that *half brother* bullshit, Hayley", Johnnie informed her. "We share the same father – the guy who earned the 'gazillion fucking dollars' to begin with. That's enough for me and since it's now *my* gazillion fucking dollars, what I choose to do with it is *my* fucking business. It's pretty black and white."

"Nothing is ever black and white", Hayley reminded him. "Remember those words? It was Brendan who articulated them when the two of you were busy rekindling your relationship."

"Well, I'm seeing more black and white than I am grey these days", Johnnie informed her. "Why are you so fucking suspicious of him?" he asked.

"Because there's a shit load of reasons to suspect he killed your parents", Hayley answered. "And if he did, maybe he doesn't think 'half' is quite enough, maybe he wants the whole thing, which puts you, and probably me, in danger."

"I'm serious, Hayley, you need to cut back on your weed consumption", Johnnie told her. "You're really starting to lose it. Brendan didn't kill my parents. Somebody did, but it wasn't him. I *know* it wasn't him."

"How do you *know* it wasn't him?" Hayley asked.

"Because I'm an absurdly good judge of character", Johnnie answered. "One thing I know is people. I know what makes them tick. That's my super power, Hayley; and I'm finally learning how to put it to good use."

"You're deluding yourself Johnnie because you want to believe everything is fantastic and you have this wonderful brother now and a new girlfriend and this amazing new life where everything is nice and tidy", Hayley went on. "That's how things work in the movies, Johnnie. That's not how they work in real life", she informed him.

"Yeah, well let me let you in on something Hayley: real life sucks; that much I'm sure of. And I just happen to have enough money to live whatever fantasy I choose", Johnnie jabbed back. "And in my fantasy I have a wonderful brother now and a new girlfriend and everything is nice and tidy. *That's* what's real for me, Hayley. That's *my* reality."

"Well then humor me, Johnnie. Let's go to the police and have them look into things. If they determine Brendan had nothing to do with your parents murders I'll never bring it up again", Hayley promised.

"Are you out of your fucking mind?" Johnnie wanted to know. "You want me to go to the police and tell them I think Brendan killed my parents even though I don't think he did? And when they ask what evidence I have I'm just supposed to say 'well, my girlfriend here has this nagging suspicion'? What the fuck, Hayley? I *like* having a brother. I'm not gonna do something stupid now to fuck that up because you're in a suspicious mood. Why can't you just let things be?"

"You're being incredibly fucking naive, Johnnie. *Incredibly* fucking naive", Hayley told him. And with that, she turned and walked away.

Johnnie wasn't quite sure what to make of Hayley's insistence that Brendan was up to no good, but he could sense that something wasn't quite right. She was reacting much too strongly and she refused to let up. In time, when people grow comfortable enough, they let their guard down and their true colors surface. "Could she still be that fucked up from what happened with her father?" he wondered. "Could that be why she's throwing all this crazy shit at me?" He was so unfazed by his own father's death that he couldn't at all relate to what Haley might have been feeling.

Brendan awoke early and headed to the train station. He was going back to Darien for a face to face with Laura and he was feeling anxious about it. He was thinking life would be a whole lot easier if people never formed relationships with each other. Relationships create obligations, obligations lead to expectations, and expectations almost always lead to disappointment. Most of the time the disappointment is unintentional, but it doesn't matter; disappointment sucks regardless of how you dress it up. Yet he knew that that was unrealistic; that it would be impossible to avoid connecting with *someone* at *some* level. It's human nature - everyone on the planet wants to feel special and appreciated. Everyone needs to feel loved. And for any of those aspirations to come to fruition you need to connect with other people. There's no way around it.

Brendan let himself into his mother's house and called for her but there was no response. He went upstairs to the bedroom where he nervously expected to find her lifeless body, the result of an overdose, or possibly a gunshot wound. Relieved that she was nowhere to be found, he went back downstairs and continued his search. As he walked into the den he found Laura sitting in Tom's recliner staring straight ahead, a blank expression on her face. He imagined a frayed piece of thread anchoring Laura's fragile soul to her body. He sensed that the thread could snap at any moment. He walked over and put his hand on her shoulder but she didn't bother to move. He thought about how he used to stand behind that chair when he was younger and apply a special potion he'd concocted to Tom's balding head in an effort to restore his youth - a repulsive combination of honey, flour, cigarette ash, salt and saliva. He remembered that Tom would sit quietly and smile while he applied it generously to the top of his skull. Who would have the nerve to betray a man that would indulge his child out of pure love like that? He realized that it was not going to be an easy day, but he had to do what he came to do, regardless of how painful it would be.

Brendan gently shook Laura's shoulder and whispered her name several times, gradually reeling her back into the moment. Looking up, she saw her son standing there, his coat still on and a concerned look in his eyes. "Brendan! When did you get here?" Laura wanted to know.

"A little while ago mom", Brendan replied. "Are you okay?"

"Yes dear, I'm fine" Laura lied. "And what about you? Are *you* okay?"

"I'm fine. Can I get you a glass of water or something?" Brendan offered.

"Yes, that would be nice. Thank you, sweetheart", Laura replied.

Brendan handed Laura the glass and took off his coat. As he sat down on the couch next to the recliner, Laura shot a quizzical gaze his way. "So, to what do I owe this pleasure?" Laura inquired. "And please, tell me; is this a visit from a kind Brendan who loves his mother, or a mean Brendan who came here to hurt her feelings again?"

"Brendan hates when you talk in the third person like that, Laura", he replied. "He thinks there's something very condescending about it."

"Well, please tell him she doesn't mean to be condescending, she's only trying to understand why he's here", Laura requested.

"Is Brendan no longer welcome here?" he wanted to know, playing along against his better judgement.

"Brendan is always welcome here", Laura said, a bit confused. "This is his home."

"Actually, that's one of the things we need to talk about, mom", Brendan informed her as he slipped back into first person mode. "I've purchased an apartment in the city. I'll be staying with my brother until I can move in, which will be in a few weeks if all goes well."

"Staying with your brother? What does that mean?" Laura asked.

"It means John Reinhartsen, Jr and I had a nice heart to heart a while back", Brendan said. "We shared lots and lots of information with each other. He was a little surprised at first to find out he had a brother, but he adjusted pretty quickly. We even had a DNA test to confirm it and, guess what – it was an exact match between me, Jr and Sr."

"But you promised to never say anything about that", Laura reminded him.

"I promised never to say anything about it while Tom McAvoy was still alive, but that's no longer an issue now, is it mother?" Brendan half asked, half accused.

"Well, what do you mean you've purchased and apartment?" Laura needed to understand. "You don't have any money of your own. Where would you get the money to buy an apartment in New York City?"

"That happens to be an incorrect statement as well", Brendan explained. "Once we confirmed that we were in fact brothers, Johnnie had no problem transferring half of his assets over to me. I'm independently wealthy now, so from this point on I'll be living on my own, making decisions for myself."

"Brendan, you're barely 19 years old. I've taken care of you your whole life", Laura said, expressing concern. "You don't know *how* to live on your own."

"Something tells me it's not that complicated, especially when you have the right funding", Brendan replied.

"Well, what about me?" Laura asked. "How am I supposed to manage on my own?"

"You've got dad's accounts now", Brendan reminded her. "You yourself said there was more than enough money to live comfortably for the rest of your life. If for some reason you need help financially, I'll be there."

"And what happens when I need help emotionally", Laura wondered. "Who do I turn to then?"

"It's too bad Big John is gone", Brendan said without skipping a beat, wanting to cause Laura pain. "He would have been the ideal guy to turn to now given how he was there for you in the past."

"Why must you be so mean to me, Brendan? I only ever wanted what was best for you", Laura said in a pathetic tone.

"I'm still trying to figure out why you felt the need to tell me any of that to begin with", Brendan replied coldly. "Do you have any idea how much that affected me over the past couple of years? And I wouldn't be surprised if Dad had something to do with what happened to Big John and Jacquie after what you did to him, by the way."

"That's not true!" Laura shouted. "Your father would never hurt anyone. And if he did, it certainly wouldn't be *my* fault. That's not fair Brendan."

"Cause and effect, Laura. It would be every bit your fault if it turned out that that's what really happened. For every action there's a reaction. I learned that in basic chemistry," Brendan explained. "Oh, and speaking of school, you should know I won't be going to Georgetown in September. Or ever, for that matter."

"You have to go to school!" Laura shrieked. "How will you ever make anything of yourself without a college education?"

"I think as far as 'making something of myself', I'm pretty much done", Brendan told her. "If I went to school for a thousand years I wouldn't earn what I already have, so what's the point?"

"The point is you'll never succeed at anything without a college education", Laura reiterated, more confused now than she was even a minute ago.

"Okay, you're just not getting it. Let's drop it", Johnnie suggested. "It's not open for discussion anyway."

"Okay, honey. Don't forget to put all your toys away and take a nice bath before dinner", Laura told him. "I'm making your favorite –steak and mashed potatoes. And corn on the Cobb! It's almost ready so don't waste any time dawdling. And let your father know, too."

Holy shit, Brendan thought to himself. She's either heavily drugged up right now or she's completely lost her fucking mind. "Mom, Dad's not here. He's gone. And it's only ten o'clock in the morning." Brendan reminded her.

"Oh that's right, dear", she laughed. "I completely forgot - he went to Boston for a few days, or was it San Francisco? Seems he's travelling more now than ever, he's hardly around anymore. We'll save him some leftovers! Now, get moving!"

"Okay mom, sounds good", Brendan told her. What else could he say? It appeared she was orbiting some

distant planet of her own now. He hoped she'd at least
find some comfort there. But he knew if this turned out to
be a permanent affliction he'd have to make other living
arrangements for Laura. "Time will tell", he thought.
"Goddamn, how much more fucking fucked up can things
get?"

"Come on Hayley, I don't want to fight with you",
Johnnie pleaded. "This is getting crazy. At this point it
doesn't matter anymore who killed my parents. They're
gone, and I don't miss them anyway. But Brendan's not
going anywhere anytime soon so you need to get your
head around that and deal with it. It will all work out fine,
trust me."

Hayley sat on the bed listening as Johnnie spoke. She
did trust him, that wasn't the issue. The issue was she
didn't trust *or* like Brendan for her own selfish reasons. She
didn't want him hanging around and getting more and
more ingrained in their lives. Ever since her father died
she's had trouble connecting with people and trusting
them. As she grew older the problem grew worse. It's
impossible to comprehend the profound effect the death of
a parent has on a small child, particularly when the child
worshiped that parent. It sometimes takes years but
almost always manifests itself in a negative way. Hayley
didn't want anyone or anything interfering with the first
genuine connection she'd made since William Mullany
passed. She was reaching her breaking point regarding

Brendan and Johnnie wasn't buying into her argument so it was time for her to go all in if she had any hope of squeezing Brendan out of the picture. Either put up or shut up. That was an expression Bill Mullany used to direct at his sons whenever they made promises he knew they'd never keep. It felt good for Hayley to say those words to herself. It gave her the feeling that her father was watching over her, guiding her. She knew what she had to do; she just needed to think things through more methodically. She calculated a very slim margin of error because if things did go bad, the consequences for her would be significant.

That night Johnnie dreamed about his mother again, only this time she was a young, healthy Jacqueline Reinhartsen. She was sitting on a chaise lounge near the pool with a cocktail in her hand, smiling. But it was a smile he didn't recognize. It dawned on him that this incarnation of his mother was one he didn't know; this was his mom before she was his mom - a pre-marriage Jacquie who had not yet succumbed to the unreasonable demands that alcohol would later impose upon her. In the dream, Jacquie greeted Johnnie with a pleasant "Hello sweetheart! You must be terribly hot after doing all that yard work. Why don't you throw on a suit and jump in the pool." Johnnie, not even the least bit warm before Jacquie mentioned the heat, suddenly felt the perspiration pouring off of his body. It was at that moment that he realized he was dreaming and yet, somehow, he was completely lucid.

"Jacquie?" Johnnie queried.

"You mean 'mom'?" Jacquie replied.

"Ok – MOM? Why do you look so young?" Johnnie wanted to know. "And *healthy*? You're supposed to be dead."

"I *am* dead", Jacquie informed him. "Dead in the realm that *your* consciousness normally operates in, anyway. You're just here for a quick visit. I wanted to let you know I'm around if you need me. I know things have been pretty intense for you since your father and I crossed over."

"I'm definitely dreaming", Johnnie thought to himself.

"Of *course* you're dreaming, John; that's why you're able to see me and talk to me", Jacquie went on.

"But I don't get it. Is this real? Me seeing and talking to you like this?" Johnnie asked. "And how did you know what I was thinking, anyway?"

"In one sense it's all very real", she explained. "You're functioning on a different level at the moment, on a different plain of existence. You're able to gain access to this realm only when your conscious mind is at rest, as it is now; or when you're meditating deeply. It's too much for your 'wide-awake' mind - and I use that term loosely - to comprehend. In case you hadn't notice, you haven't opened your mouth once since we set eyes upon each other. We're communicating telepathically. That's how it's done outside of the physical realm."

"What do you mean 'outside of the physical realm'?" Johnnie wanted to know. "I'm looking right at you. And I can see and feel my own body as well. How is that not physical?"

"It's an illusion, Johnnie", Jacquie went on. "Your brain demands these little tricks in order for it to make sense of things."

"Okay, well then maybe you can help me make sense of why you sucked so bad at being my mother while you were 'in the physical realm'", Johnnie suggested.

"I wasn't very good at parenting when I was a physical being and I'm very sorry for that, John", she confessed. "That's a weakness I need to rectify. By the same token, you *chose* to be born into that situation because there are challenges specific to your being that you need to work through as well. That's the real meaning of 'free will', by the way. It's your *choice* to be human, to continue developing your soul until it reaches its full potential. But once you become human, you also become exposed to a myriad of circumstances, both good and bad, that are created to help you strengthen the under-developed aspects of your core being. It may all seem random, and it certainly isn't easy, but there *is* a rhyme and a reason to all of it. It's about spiritual evolution, Johnnie; about coming to better know and understand the Creator, whom you refer to as 'God'. Your conscious mind probably won't remember much, if any, of this when you wake up, but you'll retain it all in your subconscious memory. When you need to call upon it, it will always be there. Being human is a struggle, John. It's designed to be. But you need to understand that the more difficult things are for you now, the more gratifying they'll be later. You need to know and understand discordance before you can truly appreciate harmony. It's about balance - the Yin and the Yang. But eventually you'll know nothing of pain and sadness. Instead, you will experience feelings of peace and contentment that are beyond your wildest dreams."

Johnny was full of questions for his mother but for some reason he was whipped back into mortal consciousness before he could get to them. He lay in bed, perfectly still, trying to figure out what the fuck had just happened. It was all so real. But it couldn't be real, could it?

Hayley was up and out of the house early the next morning. Now that she was no longer lap-dancing all night and sleeping all day she finally had the time to get back into her art in earnest, which was something she'd been hoping to do for months. But first she needed to replenish her supplies, the last of which she'd used to paint that portrait of Johnnie on the futon.

Upon returning home she'd stopped to pick up her mail, which she hadn't checked for quite a while. As she rifled through the unrelenting flow of catalogs and junk mail that she imagined must have figured out how to reproduce inside her mailbox, she noticed a small card had freed itself from the pile and fallen to the floor. Upon further inspection she saw a police emblem on the front. As she turned the card over she found a note that read "please call me when you get this card."

"What the fuck could this possibly be about", she thought as she tucked the card into the pocket of her jeans. When she got to her apartment she put the supplies down on the floor, walked over to the fridge and grabbed a cold bottle of water. Although every one of her neurons fired out a simultaneous warning to abort the mission, she picked up the phone and dialed the number anyway.

"This is Det. Dellanno, how can I help you?" a voice answered.

"This is Hayley Mullany. I found your business card in my mailbox with a note to call you, so I'm calling you", she said. "Is everything alright?"

"Ah, thank you for getting back to me, Miss Mullany. Everything's fine, I just have a few questions for you regarding an incident that occurred at the club you work at a few nights ago", the detective informed her.

"Did that man die?" she asked nervously.

"No, no; he's going to be fine. But my boss wants me to look into it so I'm looking into it", he said. "Would it be too much of an inconvenience for you to come down to the station house to answer a few questions, say tomorrow morning?"

"Why can't you ask me what you need to know right now over the phone", Hayley wondered.

"Standard police procedure, Miss Mullany" the detective informed her. "We prefer face to face conversations when conducting an investigation."

"But I had nothing to do with it. I was just doing my job", Hayley replied defensively.

"I'm not saying that you did, but you were there, and in close proximity to the altercation", Dellanno continued. "Please, come down to the station house tomorrow morning. It shouldn't take more than half an hour or so. Does 9 a.m. work for you?"

"I suppose so", Hayley replied. "Where is this station house of yours?"

"16 Ericsson Place, between Varick and Beach Street, Ma'am - the 1st Precinct. See you in the morning", Dellanno said. "And thanks for your cooperation."

"I haven't cooperated with anything yet", she thought to herself as she hung up the phone. She thought it best not to mention anything to Johnnie until she had a better handle on what this was all about.

Brendan walked into Johnnie's apartment at 10:00 a.m. after having spent the night in Connecticut. Although he was still mad as hell with his mom he wanted to make sure she was okay before heading back to the city.

"Get lucky last night, Bro?" Johnnie asked Brendan.

"That's a horrible fucking thought considering I spent the night alone with my mother at her house", Brendan informed him. "Turns out she was all fucked up from some antidepressant she was taking too much of, hallucinating that I was still a little kid and that Tom was still alive."

"You say that like it's a bad thing", Johnnie replied. "She figured out a way to hang out with the happy moments living inside her head. We should all be so lucky, although for me that would add up to a lifespan of about eight minutes."

"This is all so fucked up, John", Brendan lamented. "How did I go from living this storybook fucking life a couple of years ago, to living inside a fucking reality TV show now? I'm sure Laura's gonna need to have some sort of aid living with her full time before too long. There's no way she's gonna make it on her own and I don't have it in me to take care of her. She's responsible for fucking up our family and I really don't want anything to do with her anymore."

"That's kind of harsh, dude", Johnnie let him know. "People fuck up all the time. You can't write somebody off just because they made a mistake."

"We're not talking about a minor league error here, Johnnie; she fucked up big", Brendan said emphatically. "She banged your father, who in turn became my father, compelling Tom to drive his car off a cliff; and felt the need to tell her sixteen year old son all about it, just to clear her conscience. Dude, that's Mookie Wilson's weak little grounder rolling under Bill Buckner's glove and into right field big."

"Who the fuck is Mookie Bruckner and what's he got to do with any of this?" Johnnie wanted to know.

"You're fucking pathetic sometimes, Bro. I'm taking a shower", Brendan said as he walked out of the room.

"Don't be condenscendin' me, motherfucker", Johnnie mumbled underneath his breath as he picked up his MacBook and googled "Bucky Mookner".

CHAPTER TEN

Hayley had no problem keeping her early morning appointment with Det. Dellanno. She even showed up half an hour early as she happened to be wide-awake since 5:30 a.m., unsure of what to expect at the allotted hour. She just wanted to get it over with. So she sat in the morning call room wearing sweats and a tank top and endured the stares and comments of New York's finest while waiting for Dellanno to come and rescue her: "Welcome to the 1st Precinct miss, how can I hump you, I mean help you", one of them said. "I think I dreamed about you last night, but I can't tell through all those cloths you're wearing", said another. "Just say the word and Office Igivuluv will be at you service in an instant", a third one offered.

"They're good guys", Det. Dellanno said as he escorted Hayley upstairs to the squad room, admiring the view from behind as he spoke.   "They're just a little bit immature."

"A *little bit* immature?" Hayley responded with surprise. "That's like saying the Pope is a *little bit* Catholic."

"Don't sweat it, they don't mean any harm", Dellanno assured her.

"I'm used to it, actually", Hayley said in a less exaggerated tone now. "You can't be in my former profession and be squeamish about men ogling you and passing lewd comments. That's the curse of extreme beauty, or so I've been told", she joked.

"I suppose so, but I'll try to keep my lewd comments to a bare minimum. The ogling I can't make any promises about. So you're out of the business now, you mentioned?" Dellanno asked.

"Well, they shit-canned me downtown so now I'm black listed due to the violent nature of the crime. I couldn't work in the business again even if I wanted to", Hayley went on. "Fortunately, I no longer want to."

"So, what's a nice girl like you gonna do for a living now?" the detective probed. "You know, the police exam is coming up, we could use more good women on the job."

"Ha! My father was FDNY! He'd roll over in his grave if I became one of you", Hayley explained. "Not that I have any desire to be a cop. I'm an artist, detective. And a good one at that. I was dancing to earn money until I hit it big. Now I can concentrate on something I'm truly passionate about rather than having to fake it for twenty bucks a pop."

"I can see that your art means a lot to you. You got this little sparkle in your eye just then when you started talking about it", Det. Dellanno said. "I was at the Met recently for the Cezanne exhibit. I'm a big fan of the early Impressionists. Of course both Cezanne and Gauguin were later categorized as 'Post-Impressionist Masters", but each got their start during the early Impressionist's movement."

"Well, thank you for the art history lesson, Detective", Hayley said. "I am seriously impressed. I didn't figure you to be such an aficionado."

"Oh, really?" Dellanno said, feigning insult. "Is that because I'm just a dumb cop? You know, you have to have at least a modicum of intelligence to become detective first grade, Ms Mullany."

"I suppose your right, detective. I'm sorry; I didn't mean to insult you", Hayley apologized.

"Ah, you didn't insult me. I was just messin' around", Dellanno told her. "But I *am* an art enthusiast. And *you* should be more careful about judging people before you know anything about them. You're right; you'd never make it as a detective."

"Oh, I never said I couldn't make it; what I said was I had no interest in playing cops and robbers, which you would have heard had you actually been listening to what I was saying as opposed to staring at my tits", Hayley replied.

"Pardon, Mademoiselle", Dellanno replied with a near-perfect French accent. "I was so captivated by your extreme beauty that I must have missed it. While I still have un petit peu of my wit intact, perhaps we should turn to the matter at hand."

"That's why I'm here, detective. Shoot", she said. "And please, don't take that literally."

"Best be careful how y'all say things to a dumb-ass cop like me, y'all could get hurt", Dellanno played along.

"So, the 'gentleman' that smashed the bottle across your customer's face – I'm assuming you know him?"

"You're assumption is correct, detective", Hayley replied.

"Would you care to elaborate on that, Ms Mullany?" Dellanno asked.

"Not really, Dick. That *is* still slang for 'detective', is it not?" Hayley goaded.

"It was, a long time ago. These days people just refer to us as assholes", Dellanno admitted. "So, I should probably tell you that whoever that was that cracked the big man that night is wanted for assault with a deadly weapon, which just happens to be a felony in this cosy little jurisdiction of ours. That's jail time, Hayley. No laughing matter. What's the guy's name and address? Now that you've told me you know him, you could be found an accessory to a violent felony for withholding information. That would mean jail time for you as well. Is this guy your boyfriend or something?"

"He's just a friend", Hayley told him. "But I don't want him going to jail. He's a good guy and he thought he was defending my honor. Isn't there some other way we can handle this?"

"Not likely", the detective explained. "Listen, all kidding aside, this was an incredibly violent act. If he did it once, there's nothing to stop him from doing it again. You could be endangering yourself if you don't give him up so think carefully before you respond this time. Who is he and where does he live, Hayley?"

"He'd never raise his hands to me, detective. The guy's madly in love with me", Hayley replied.

"Jesus, if I had a dollar for every time some woman uttered those very words", Dellanno responded with disgust in his voice. "I could have paid for every one of their funerals and still had enough left over to retire a very wealthy man."

"Perhaps we are being un petit dramatique, officier; oui?" Hayley asked.

"I wish that were the case, Hayley. I honestly do", Dellanno told her. "Unfortunately, the statistics don't lie."

"Well, what if I told you I had information about a different case that's much more worthy of your time than a little bottle across a face in a strip club?" Hayley offered.

"That depends", Dellanno explained. "Whaddaya got?"

"What I got is a 2 year old cold case, murder one, and a perp that looks damn good for the crime", Hayley replied in her best Law and Order cop-speak.

"Okay, slow down", Dellanno pleaded. "If I'm hearing you right, 'officer'; you're saying you have information regarding a murder that took place 2 years ago, correct?"

"Duh", Hayley replied nervously.

"Can we get serious for a moment, Hayley?" Dellanno asked once again. "If what you're telling me is on the money, we may actually be able to do something for your friend if the info pans out."

"Oh, it's on the money alright." Hayley replied.

"Good. Give me the 50,000 foot view so I can start looking into it", Dellanno requested.

"Look into the deaths of John and Jacqueline Reinhartsen of Greenwich, Connecticut. It happened about 2 years ago. That should be enough to peak your interest", Hayley told him.

"Connecticut's a little bit out of my jurisdiction, Hayley. I don't see how that's gonna help your friend", Dellanno said.

"Well the guy that did the killing is *living* in your jurisdiction now, detective", Hayley explained. "Does that help?"

"Okay. Let's keep this between me and you for now. I need to run to a meeting with my squad commander but I'll be in touch", Detective Dellanno promised. "Do you have a number I can reach you on?"

"Yes", Hayley said.

"Can you give it to me, please?" Dellanno asked.

"Sure", Hayley said with a chuckle. She gave him the number and he escorted her out of the house. As she got off the subway and walked back home she experienced a very special kind of euphoria – the kind one can only appreciate after a job well done. "Genius", she thought to herself as she entered the building.

Johnnie and Brendan were just finishing up breakfast when Hayley walked in. "Where you been, Hayley girl? I woke up this morning and you were gone", Johnny said.

"Just out running some errands, didn't want to wake you. You looked so comfortable", Hayley replied. "What are your plans for today?"

"Well", Johnnie said. "After we finish eating we thought it might be a good idea to light up a joint and ponder our existence. After much pondering, we'll likely order some more food and then eat that. *Then*, we'll probably light up another joint and reflect upon our previous ponderences. After that, it's anyone's guess. Would you care to join us?"

"As intriguing as all that sounds, I think I'm going to head downstairs and do a little painting", Hayley told the boys. "You ponder, I'll paint. See you guys later."

"I think she's finally coming around", Brendan said, somewhat surprised. "I think she's starting to like me."

"Let's not get carried away, dude", Johnnie warned. "Just because she didn't say anything nasty doesn't mean the two of you are suddenly BFF's."

"What's she got against me, anyway?" Brendan asked. "I mean, I know I came on a little strong at first, but that was before we worked our shit out. The only logical thing it could be at this point is sexual tension. That shit happens to me a lot."

"She wants you Bren, what woman doesn't?" Johnnie chimed in.

"True. I'll try and let her down easy, for your sake", Brendan offered.

"Thank you, Brendan!" Johnnie mocked. "What a good brother!"

"Just tryin' to do my part", Brendan replied. "It's all about the greater good. Can't allow self-interests to get in the way."

"You're so full of shit", Johnnie said. "If Hayley walked into the room right now wearing nothing, pointed to you and said 'your turn', you'd be on that shit before your brain even had a chance to process the data."

"Yeah, I know", Brendan admitted. "But I'd probably feel bad afterwards. That's gotta count for something, no?"

"Oh, yeah." Johnnie said. "That'd straighten things right out."

Dellanno decided to Google the murders rather than go through internal sources to see what he could come up with. He didn't want to create any unnecessary attention. If he determined he had something probable he'd talk to the squad commander about it. Until then he would conduct his research privately.

It didn't take long to track down information on the case; it was all over the Web. He browsed through a few links and then clicked on one for the Greenwich Times. He found the story immediately – it was big front page news. The article stated "John Reinhartsen Sr., the 56 year old founder and managing partner of JR Capital, a $26 Billion dollar Wall Street hedge fund, and his socialite wife, Jacqueline, 54, were found murdered in their Greenwich home yesterday by their young son, John Jr., who had returned home from a college prep course to discover the carnage. Jacqueline was found in her bed with a fractured skull and John in the garage, with a fractured skull and two broken legs." After browsing a couple of dozen other articles he came across the following: "After an extensive investigation the case was ruled a home invasion and shut down due to a lack of forensic evidence at the scene. The detective in charge of the case, Sean Mazzetti, stated he felt confident that the homicides were the result of a random act of violence." It went on to describe John and Jacquie in greater detail but Dellanno wasn't interested in any of that at the moment. He'd found what he was looking for – the name of the lead detective.

Dellanno searched the internet once again, this time for the phone number of the Greenwich police department. He dialled the number, identified himself and asked for Det. Mazzetti. "Mazzetti's been off the job for 18 months. Is there someone else who can help you", the desk sergeant asked.

"Is there anyone there that would be familiar with a double homicide that took place about two years ago? Guy and his wife got their heads bashed in, Reinhartsen was the name. The deaths were ruled the result of a home invasion", Dellanno went on.

"That case went cold a while ago. You got something new on this?" the sergeant wanted to know.

"I might have some information that could justify re-opening the case." Dellanno said.

"Interesting, if you're not pullin' my dick. You'll wanna talk to Det. Freedman. I'll put you through to him", the sergeant offered.

Dellanno waited almost a full minute until the detective picked up. "You got Freedman. Whaddaya need?" the detective answered in a whiney, agitated voice.

"This is Detective Bobby Dellanno from the 1st Precinct in Manhattan", Dellanno replied.

"And what can I do for you, *Detective*?" Freedman countered sarcastically.

"You could change the tone of your voice, for one thing", Dellanno advised.

"You got a problem with the way I'm talkin' to you *Detective*? What, is your dirty diaper making you cranky?" Freedman pushed.

"Do I know you? Are you a friend of mine?" Dellanno wanted to know. "Because only friends get to talk to me like I'm an asshole. Everyone else gets to wait in line."

"Alright, don't get your knickers in a twist. I was just fucking with you", Freedman said by way of an apology. "How can I help you, Bobby?"

"It's about how I can help you, actually", Dellanno informed him. "I've got this source yapping in my ear about a double homicide that took place in your jurisdiction a couple of years ago that your boy, Mazzetti, ruled a home invasion with no legitimate suspects due to a lack of forensics. It appears he closed the case down and ran off to Florida to live happily ever after", Dellanno said. "My source claims to have bona fide info on a high probability suspect that I think would be of interest to you. Might turn out to be nothin', but it's probably worth a couple of hours of our combined time."

"You got my attention", Freedman said. "Go on".

"Suggestion, why don't I shoot up to CT this afternoon and pick up the case file and other material pertinent to the investigation. I could use the OT anyway. I'll have a go at it and bring it back to you as soon as I connect some of the dots", Dellanno suggested. "It's tied to another felony I'm working so it's important that it looks like I'm calling the shots. This kid made it clear she will only talk to me. You ok with that, detective?" Dellanno wanted to know. "If this gets solved, your name will be all over it."

"I get it, but don't try to fuck me on this", Freedman warned. "You NYPD pricks are notorious for taking the credit and comin' off like big shots, like us small town guys don't know our dicks from our doughnuts."

"I believe the expression is 'our asses from our elbows' but no worries, pal. You have my word", Dellanno promised.

"Whatever. I'll tell the property clerk to expect you this afternoon. Just remember, if you should get cute and try to fuck me, I'll have the last laugh. I *always* have the last laugh", Freedman warned again.

"Got it, detective. You're *really* starting to scare me now so I better get going. But I'm tellin' you, if we pull this off they'll be plenty of credit to go around", Dellanno assured him.

"Then let's get it done", Freedman said. "Mazzetti was a hack who had no business running a show this big. Don't expect to find too much in that case file, he botched up the whole fucking investigation. He didn't retire of his own accord, if you know what I'm saying."

"Reading you loud and clear. Let's talk in a few days", Bobby said and hung up the phone.

Hayley stripped down in her artist's den and ran a bath. As she soaked she thought about her encounter with Bobby Dellanno. It was obvious he was into her. She realized that if she had any shot at making Brendan disappear she'd have to work Dellanno like the pro she was. "Shouldn't be that difficult", she thought. "He is a man, after all." But this chore was going to require more than just a little flirting. She was going to need to ratchet it up a few notches. The thought aroused her. "At least he's cute", she thought.

Then another thought crossed her mind. Could it be that God was allowing everything to suddenly fall into place like this because He was trying to make up with Hayley? "Why not?" she thought. "He made a mistake. It must be pretty complicated controlling everything in the entire universe all at once." While she'll never forget the pain and the sense of abandonment she experienced when her father died, she was willing to give God another chance. She was willing to be friends again.

Laura sat in her kitchen with an untouched cup of coffee in front of her on the table in the window nook. As she half watched two squirrels enacting an age old mating ritual, she thought back on some of the age old events in her own life. She thought about when she and Tom first met. She was just a kid, 19 years old, and Tom a much more mature twenty three. They were on line at a movie theatre, both of them solo, waiting to buy tickets. Tom, calling upon every ounce of courage inhabiting his body and soul, leaned over and asked a very simple question: "Did anyone ever tell you you look just like Audrey Hepburn?" he said.

Of course she'd heard that comparison many times over the years, but she was kind and told the stranger "no, but that's awfully nice of you. Audrey Hepburn is so beautiful. I only wish it were true!" she lied. She was quite aware at the age of 19 of just how beautiful she was. "No, it *is* true", Tom said. "You're the spit and image of a young Audrey Hepburn, circa 'Breakfast at Tiffany's'."

"Oh, that's one of my favorite movies in the world!" Laura gushed.

"It is a wonderful film", Tom, who had never actually seen 'Breakfast at Tiffany's' said. "Are you waiting for someone?"

"No, I'm afraid I'm on my own this evening", Laura admitted.

"How fortuitous! I'm on my own as well", Tom, feeling brave now, told Laura. "Why don't we sit together?"

'I'd love to", said Laura. "But not too close to the screen, it gives me a headache."

"Wherever you want to sit is fine with me. I'm Tom", he said with an outstretched hand.

"Hi Tom, I'm Laura", she replied. "It's a pleasure to meet you."

As she sat staring out her kitchen window more than a quarter of a century down the road in Darien, Connecticut, Laura felt tears streaming down her face. "What have I done?" she thought. "I've taken everything that meant anything to me and destroyed it all. How could I have been so selfish? Brendan was right – I had a wonderful man like Tom McAvoy sitting right here next to me and I just had to give in to that horrible beast John Reinhartsen. Yes Tom, I'm fully aware of where the nickname 'Big John' comes from. But you already knew that when you asked the question, didn't you. Oh, Tom, I'm so sorry I hurt you. I'm a terrible person and I don't deserve to be happy. Even Brendan wants nothing to do with me anymore. I've ruined everything, Tom. Everything."

And with that, she picked up the revolver that was sitting on the window seat beside her, the same one Tom had purchased so long ago to insure no one would ever inflict harm upon his family, and fired a single shot into her right temple.

CHAPTER ELEVEN

Secrets. We all have them. Oh, sure; anyone can have a run of good luck where without much effort at all your secrets can be kept at bay for months and months, even years, if you're especially lucky. But, eventually, there's going to be a knock on your door. That day of reckoning will come. And when it does, those secrets that most offend will be standing there glaring at you, daring you to run. And the longer you wait for that knock, the less prepared you'll be. You'll start to believe you're in the clear. That's when you're fucked. After all, the Grand Masters spend every waking moment of their existence concentrating on expunging the evil within and purifying their souls. And most cross over without ever accomplishing that goal. If they're lucky they get to rest for a millennium or two - the blink of an eye in the greater scheme of things - only to come back and start all over again. Who the fuck are we, those of us who treat being human as a *hobby*, to believe we're any better than the secrets we keep? Laura, Tom, Big John and Jacquie, four individuals, each one a fatality of their own opaque storyboards. Ruth and Dave, still running. But they, too, will learn that there's no such thing as a "perfect crime". Oh, what a tangled web, indeed.

*

Det. Dellanno spent the morning sifting through the box of physical evidence he brought back with him from Connecticut. He examined the bloodied Louisville slugger, still covered in Jacquie's dried blood and grey matter; the bicycle pump, coated with bits and pieces of Big John's oesophagus; 100+ crime scene photos and, of course, the case file itself. He took note of the fact that there was an alarming lack of forensic evidence at the crime scene. Whoever committed the crime knew what he was doing. In Dellanno's mind, the lack of forensics clearly indicated premeditation. He also took note after reading the file that nothing appeared to have been stolen. Big John's wallet, cash and credit cards were still in his pocket when he was found; his gazillion dollar Patek Philippe wristwatch was still on his wrist and his rings still adorned his broken fingers. Jacquie's jewellery was right where she left it. It's possible, he conceded, the intruders were scared off before they had a chance to actually take anything, but his instincts told him otherwise. A fucking 6th grader could have put these pieces together after a single pass through the crime scene. Whoever killed Big John and Jacquie went there to kill Big John and Jacquie; they weren't interested in stealing anything, or even pretending to. What the fuck was wrong with these clowns from Connecticut? They weren't even in the same league as the NYPD auxiliary police force, Dellanno thought.

Brendan's cell phone rang and rang until he was awake enough to pick it up early that Saturday morning. "Hello?" Brendan said as he wiped the sleep from his eyes.

"Brendan, its Aunt Rosanne. I've been trying to reach you", she said.

"What's up, Roro? Is everything ok", Brendan wanted to know. He could hear the trepidation in her voice.

"No sweetheart, it's not. I hadn't heard from your mother for a couple of days and I couldn't reach her by phone so Mike went over to see if everything was alright. Brendan, your mom's dead. She committed suicide. I knew she was despondent but I had no idea she was that far gone. I should have known better. I should have been there with her", Rosanne said, losing her composure.

"Slow down, Roro", Brendan demanded. "What do you mean she committed suicide? When? I mean, I was just with her. What the fuck!"

"She shot herself Brendan. The poor thing shot herself. I can't imagine what was going on in her head that would make her go to such extremes. Dear God", Rosanne said.

"Jesus Fucking Christ!" Brendan screamed. "When does this nightmare end? How could she do this, Roro? What am I supposed to do now? Now I don't have a father *or* a mother. Jesus Christ. At least I have a brother", Brendan said.

"What do you mean 'at least you have a brother'?" Rosanne asked. "You know?"

"I know. I've known about what my mother did for a long time", Brendan informed his aunt.

"Does that mean that John knows, too?" Rosanne asked.

"Johnnie knows", Brendan told her. "We've worked things out though and we're good with each other. He even transferred half his inheritance over to me. I bought an apartment in the city and will be living there from now on. What am I supposed to do about my mother, Roro? I don't even know how to make funeral arrangements. I don't know how to do anything. I'm a fucking orphan now. Jesus Christ!"

"You're not alone, Brendan", Rosanne offered. "I know it feels like you are, but you're not. Uncle Mike and I are here for you, always. Your mom was sick, Brendan. She had lots of stuff going on inside her head that she just couldn't figure out how to cope with anymore. She was a tortured soul, Bren. Not many people know that, but it's true. Your father did everything he could to accommodate her afflictions and support her. He loved her so much, Brendan. Life is tricky, honey, and you've seen too much of the bad side of it already. But you have to keep in mind that it's not always going to be that way. There's a lifetime of happy moments in front of you still. Don't let the hard times weigh you down. Be strong, honey. And figure out a way to be happy."

"You sound just like my father now. That's exactly what he used to tell me", Johnnie told his aunt. "What am I supposed to do about the funeral arrangements?"

"Mike and I will handle everything, Bren. I'll call you in a day or two to update you. In the meantime, you call us whenever you need to. Do you want to come and spend a few days with us until things settle down?" Rosanne asked. "It might do you some good to be around your family."

"No thanks, Roro" Brendan said. "I'll be ok. It's just gonna take a while to get used to all of this. It's all my fault. I was such a shit to her since my father died, blaming her for everything. I should've known better."

"Brendan, you need to understand something. What happened with your mother is the end result of a lifetime of mental illness. That has nothing to do with you. You were a wonderful son and she loved you very much", Rosanne informed him.

"What do you mean mental illness? Was she crazy???" Brendan needed to understand.

"Not crazy, but her brain didn't work the way a normal brain is supposed to. She was ok when she was young but as she got older the problem grew worse. She had trouble distinguishing between what was real and what wasn't. It's a form of schizophrenia."

"I've got to go now, Roro. I've got a lot of stuff to figure out. Thank you for handling this and I'll talk to you in a couple of days. I love you."

"I love you too, Brendan. Very much", Rosanne let him know as she hung up the phone.

Det. Dellanno shuffled through the papers on his desk until he'd found what he was looking for - the piece with Hayley's phone number on it. As he dialled the number he thought about how beautiful she was. It was hard not to.

"Hello", Hayley said as she picked up her cell phone in the studio.

"Hayley, its Detective Dellanno" the detective said, trying to hide the excitement in his voice. He felt like he was 13 again, calling to ask Joanne Burns to the 8th grade dance. "Listen, I've been going through the evidence I picked up in Connecticut yesterday and what really stands out is the fact that good, solid police work is completely missing from the investigation. From what I can see this was in no way a home invasion. I think it's time for you to share with me the details of what you know. Can we get together today? Maybe meet outside the neighborhood for coffee?"

"Why detective! Are you asking me out on a date?" Hayley flirted.

"Ms. Mullany, I assure you I am a consummate professional", Dellanno replied with mock astonishment. "My request to meet with you lies strictly within the context of official police business."

"Whatever you say, detective. When and where would you like to meet?" Hayley asked.

"Let's meet downtown in an hour. There's a little diner on Barclay Street, right across from the Woolworth building off Broadway. The 1 train stops a block away at

Park Place. A buddy of mine owns the place, an ex-cop. Brilliant investigator. I wouldn't mind having him sit in on the conversation and getting his two cents on the whole thing", Dellanno informed her.

"Fine with me, Bobby", Hayley replied. "Oh, I'm sorry detective; is it alright for me to call you 'Bobby'? I wouldn't want to overstep my bounds when it comes to 'official police business', after all", she teased.

"Well, the name on my birth certificate is actually 'Robert', but my friends have always called me 'Bobby'." Dellanno replied. "You can call me whatever you like."

"I still think 'Dick' has a nice ring to it, but I'll go with Bobby", she said, tongue in cheek.

"Fine by me. I'll see you in an hour, *Hayley*", Dellanno replied.

"Looking forward to it, *Bobby*", Hayley said, turning up the flirt.

Brendan walked into Johnnie's room and woke him. Johnnie wasn't happy. "Dude, you're not gonna believe this", Brendan baited his brother.

"Another Brendan mystery, how unusual", Johnnie answered sarcastically.

"This one isn't exactly mysterious, just sad", Brendan replied.

"What happened now?" Johnnie wanted to know.

"Your prediction came true, John. We're both orphans now", Brendan informed him. "My mother shot herself a couple of days ago. My aunt just called to let me know. Apparently she's had a history of mental illness that goes way back to when she was a kid. I never had any idea, but it does explain a lot", Brendan said. "Tom knew all about it and tried his best to help her cope. Having that affair with the Magic Lady must have fucked up his head so bad that he just couldn't live with himself anymore. The guy was a saint. And I, of course, had to be a little prick and make my mother feel like it was all her fault that he killed himself. I basically pushed her to commit suicide."

"Fuck, Bren. I'm really sorry", Johnnie offered. "You're having like the worst run ever right now. What can I do to help?

"Nothing at the moment, Bro", Brendan let him know. "Just need to let all this shit sink in. It's so ridiculous at this point that I don't even feel bad. In fact, I don't feel anything."

"That's ok. It's just your brains way of trying to cope with the stress. You've lost both your parents within a week of each other under horrible circumstances, and you're still trying to deal with the fact that you suddenly have a brother", Johnnie went on. "You'll figure it all out, it'll just take time. Don't make things worse by putting any of this shit on yourself. You didn't contribute to anything. Your mom and dad had their own reasons for doing what they did. And they didn't have anything to do with you."

"I guess. It's all so hazy right now", Brendan admitted. "The only part that actually

makes any sense to me at all is that you and I are brothers. At least that's one thing I can be thankful for. It doesn't even feel weird anymore."

"You're right about that, dude; I feel the same way", Johnnie conferred. "Let's go out and get something to eat. Maybe get a little stoned first?"

"Yeah, I could use something to take the edge off. Got anything handy?" Brendan asked.

"Need to roll some up. You know where everything is. Why don't you take care of that while I take a quick shower", Johnnie suggested.

As Johnnie walked into the bathroom, Brendan walked into his bedroom, laid down on the bed and wept like a little boy. "Jesus Christ, how much more fucking fucked up can things get."

CHAPTER TWELVE

Hayley met Det. Dellanno at the diner an hour after they hung up the phone. She spotted him immediately sitting with his ex-cop-diner-owning friend, a gigantic human being, in a booth toward the back of the restaurant. Bobby looked up and waved her over.

"Good morning Hayley, meet my friend Roger Parrino. Roger is an ex-homicide detective. In fact, he used to run all of Manhattan North, so he's got a lot of experience catching bad guys who kill people", Dellanno informed her.

"Pleasure to meet you, Ms. Mullany", Parrino told her. "Please have a seat. Can I offer you some coffee or tea?"

Hayley returned the greeting. "Coffee would be great, thank you."

"My pleasure", Parrino assured her. He motioned for the waiter to come over. "So, Bobby tells me your spidey senses have been tingling lately over a double homicide that took place up in Greenwich a couple of years ago. I remember that case. Husband and wife beat with a bat, no apparent motive. Guy was some hedge fund mogul and his wife a socialite. The lead detective must have gotten bored after a few months and shut the case down due to a lack of evidence. Based on what Bobby has said, I'd have to agree that this looks a lot more like Murder One than it does some random home invasion."

"I'd have to agree, too", Hayley said, "particularly since I know who killed them."

"That's a pretty serious statement to make with so much conviction behind it", Parrino warned. Hayley smiled to herself thinking what Johnnie would have said had he witnessed this outburst of decisiveness on her part.

"Yeah, well after you hear what I'm about to say I'd be shocked if you didn't feel the same way", Hayley informed the rather large man sitting in front of her.

"Hayley, it's important that you don't leave anything out", Dellanno told her. "Take your time and be very deliberate. Keep in mind that what you say here this morning will have a very profound effect on another person's life, so choose your words carefully."

"I'll keep that in mind, detective", Hayley replied with a smirk.

"I'm serious, Hayley, this is no joke", Dellanno scolded. "Someone could be put away for the rest of their life based, in part, upon what you say today; so don't make any statements or accusations unless you're extremely confident in what you have to say."

"Got it, Dick....OOPS! I meant to say 'detective'", Hayley continued. Dellanno didn't like that Hayley was being so flippant about such a serious matter and was thinking of calling the interview off, but stopped short of actually saying the words. He had the feeling she was showing off for Parrino, which, of course, she was.

The coop board in Johnnie's building did something completely out of the ordinary for NYC cooperative boards –they green lighted Brendan to proceed with the purchase of his apartment inside of a week and informed him he could move in as soon as the final paperwork was completed. Unheard of. The fact that he didn't need to apply and wait for a mortgage certainly worked in his favor. Brendan had about 3 days to shop for and rush order furniture if he intended to move in any time soon. So he and Johnnie went down to Restoration Hardware and ordered just about every piece of furniture and accessory Brendan would need. Money, of course, was no object. Not only did Brendan share in Big John's fortune, he was now in possession of Tom's vast wealth, too. But he hadn't lost sight of what his father had told him over and over again throughout his childhood: he was obliged to give back. And he intended to.

"Ok Hayley, time to get down to business", Dellanno said. "If you've got information on this case, why don't you let Roger and me in on it?"

"OK Bobby. I'm sorry; I didn't mean to be so obnoxious. I'm a little nervous, I guess", Hayley admitted.

"No worries, Hayley. Let's just start from the beginning and take things nice and slow", Dellanno guided her. Parrino shot his friends a quick look that said "put your dick back in your pants and screw your fucking head on straight."

"Alright, here goes", Hayley replied with a deep breath. "I met this guy Johnnie a while back while I was walking through Central Park one sunny morning at around 11 a.m. After talking for a while we realized we lived in the same building."

"Does Johnnie have a last name?" Parrino wondered.

"He does. It's the same as those poor people that were murdered in Greenwich. They were his parents," Hayley confirmed.

"Interesting", Parrino said. "Go on."

"Well at first I didn't know that. When I asked him what he did for a living he told me he was a writer, and that his name was John Cook", Hayley went on. "When I asked what he was writing about he said it was a story about a young boy who killed his parents to inherit their fortune."

"Are you suggesting that this kid, Johnnie, killed his parents, Hayley?" Parrino wanted to know.

"No, not at all", Hayley was quick to correct him. "He later informed me that he lied; that he wasn't a writer at all. He claimed to be living off of some huge trust fund his grandfather left him. Turned out he was living off the inheritance from his parents."

"Why do you think he lied about it to begin with?" Parrino asked.

"He just didn't know me, so he didn't trust me with the truth", Hayley continued. "Once we got to know each other he told me everything. Told me he hated his parents and didn't care that they were dead. Said he was better off without them and that whoever killed them did him a favor."

"Where was Johnnie at the time of the murders? Did he ever mention that?" Parrino wanted to know.

"Taking some college prep course at the time. When he got home he found his mom dead in her bed", Hayley said.

"That's what the papers said, too", Dellanno agreed. "Sounds like he's got a pretty tight alibi. Those records are easy to check – even the Greenwich PD would have thought to have done that."

"Yeah, but even if Johnnie can prove he wasn't there at the time of the murders, that doesn't exactly let him off the hook. He could have arranged to have a third party do it at that specific time when he knew he'd have solid air cover, particularly after what you just told us about his relationship with his parents", Parrino informed her.

"Nah, Johnnie's not a murderer. He doesn't have it in him", Hayley said.

"I think the big man in the strip club would beg to differ", Dellanno said. "We all have it in us somewhere; it's just a matter of what brings it to the surface. Johnnie could easily have killed that guy at the club and, in fact, came close to doing so."

"I really didn't come here to talk about Johnnie", Hayley said, a bit flustered now. "I came here to talk about his brother, Brendan."

"What brother? All the reports have Johnnie as an only child. Where does a brother suddenly come into the picture?" Dellanno wanted to know.

"About a month ago this guy shows up out of the blue and starts talking to Johnnie like they're old friends. Johnnie clearly knows him but doesn't want anything to do with him. Turns out their families used to socialize when they were little – Brendan's dad worked for Johnnie's dad – and it was clear Brendan was here for something. He didn't just stumble upon Johnnie", Hayley said as she paused to catch her breath. "I got up and left because I figured they needed some privacy, so I went back to my place to wait for him. When Johnnie got home he looked like he'd just gotten some special news directly from God." Hayley paused once again, this time for effect.

"And what kind of news did the Good Lord share with Johnnie that day", Parrino asked.

"That Johnnie's dad knocked up Brendan's mom, who in turn gave birth to a son, whom she called Brendan", Hayley replied. "Johnnie walked out of his apartment that morning an only child and came home a sibling."

"And how did Johnnie feel about that?" Dellanno asked.

"Surprisingly, he felt pretty good about it", Hayley informed the detectives. "I, on the other hand saw right through what was going on."

"Which was?" Parrino questioned.

"Which was that Brendan came down to scam half of Johnnie's inheritance out from under him, which is exactly what I told Johnnie he was doing and which is exactly what he did."

"So you're saying that this kid, Brendan, walks in off the street, says 'hey, I'm your half brother. How 'bout giving me half your inheritance', and that was that?" Dellanno asked.

"No, not quite that easy. Johnnie insisted they get a DNA test and Brendan happily went along with it. Science corroborated his story", Hayley told them.

"So, if I'm hearing you right you're suggesting that Brendan killed Johnnie's parents so he could get his fair share of the inheritance and he may even have done so to avenge the death of his real father , the guy that raised him. Did Brendan's father know about the affair and the biological consequence?" Bobby asked.

"He did. He admitted it in the suicide note he left for Brendan", Hayley advised.

"And when did this guy commit suicide?" Bobby wanted to know.

"A few weeks ago", Hayley said, matter-of-factly.

"Sounds to me like we've got a host of characters that could foot the bill from a circumstantial perspective", Dellanno said as Parrino listened and nodded in agreement. "We've got Johnnie, who hated his parents and stood as the sole heir to their fortune; we've got

Brendan's father, who was wronged in the worst imaginable way by his friend and boss and then couldn't live with himself afterwards; we've got Brendan's mom, who's own guilt in the matter could have driven her to extremes; and we've got Brendan, looking to avenge his dad and pick up a substantial fortune for his efforts. What we don't appear to have, however, is one single piece of physical evidence linking any of them to the crime. No judge is going to re-open a case like this based on circumstantial evidence."

"Well I'd be looking hard at Brendan if I were you", Hayley suggested. "For one thing he admitted to Johnnie that he'd spent weeks figuring out how to get even with Johnnie's father. He knew at the time of the Reinhartsen's death that Big John was his biological father. It killed him to think that piece of shit could betray the man who raised him and think he could get away with it."

"How did Brendan know all this?" Parrino asked.

"His mother sat him down and told him – *before* the murders. He knew all about it before they were killed. He's a cocky fuck who could very easily have convinced himself he could get away with it", Hayley went on. Brendan's dad was a mild –mannered guy who went out and had an affair to get even with his wife. In the end, that's what did him in. Brendan's mother apparently suffered with mental illness since she was a kid. Johnnie wasn't a fighter and he certainly didn't have it in him to brutally beat his parents to death. Having hung out with these two guys for a coupla months now I'd say your most likely suspect is Brendan McAvoy. I believe Brendan's dangerous and that he won't be satisfied with half of his brother's fortune. That puts both Johnnie and me in danger. Isn't what I've told you enough to pick him up and question him?"

"Probably not", Parrino said. "But why don't you let us think about it for a little while and we'll get back to you with our thoughts and probably some more questions."

"Ok, thanks for taking this seriously", Hayley said.

"Listen, this isn't so far-fetched. You present a reasonable argument. He certainly had motive and opportunity", Parrino assured her. "As Bobby said, physical evidence would go a long, long way in supporting your argument. Let us see if we could come up with enough reasons to bring him in and maybe do a search of his place. Where does he live?" Parrino asked.

"He just bought an apartment in the building Johnnie and I live in. I think he's planning on moving in this weekend", Hayley said.

"Perfect. Maybe we can take a peek around while things are in disarray. I look forward to following up with you", Parrino admitted. "Bobby, let's talk tomorrow.

"Sounds good, Cap. Thanks for your help", Bobby said.

"Once a cop......" Parrino let the thought trail off.

*

Hayley jumped in the car with Dellanno before she was even asked. "Upper west side please, and step on it", she joked.

"No problem miss", Dellanno played along. "I just hope you have enough to pay your way. I don't take kindly to freeloaders."

"I can *always* pay my way, driver. You just keep your eyes on the road and your hands upon the wheel", Hayley demanded.

"Doors. Roadhouse Blues", Dellanno replied with mild astonishment. "You're too young to know that song Hayley. Where'd that come from?"

"I'm the youngest of six children detective. My oldest brother Terry cranked the Doors from the moment he woke up in the morning to the moment he passed out at night. Used to drive my father crazy. I'm a big fan of the music from that era", Hayley informed Bobby.

"Are you sure you're only twenty two?" Bobby asked rhetorically.

"Chronologically, yes. Experientially, I'm well beyond that", Hayley replied.

"You are something else, kid", Bobby mindlessly spat out. "I'll drop you a few blocks away on Columbus so no one sees you getting out of the car."

"Ok, that works. Listen Bobby", Hayley said. "I'm really serious about Brendan. The guy's a scammer and a mean son-of-a-bitch. I'm afraid of him and I want him gone. Please help me with this Bobby. Please?"

"Hayley, I promise I'll do everything I can do within the scope of the law. If he's guilty, we'll nail him. But it's gonna take time. For one thing, other jurisdictions don't like when outsiders get involved and make them look bad, so we're not gonna get any cooperation from the Greenwich PD, or even the State Police for that matter. This has got to be handled delicately every step of the way", Bobby lectured.

"I know you'll do what's right, Bobby. I'll talk to you later", Hayley said as she leaned over to give him a peck on the cheek. As the corners of their mouths brushed against each other, so did their tongues and what ensued inside Bobby's unmarked patrol car was the kind of stuff you see in those cop movies from the early 70's when the sleep deprived detective is questioning the beautiful hooker in his filthy black Dodge Charger about a murder she witnessed and the next thing you know it's all nudity and adult situations. Fortunately, they managed to regain their composure before things got too out of hand in broad daylight on crowded Columbus Avenue. But Bobby took the bait and the hook was set. All Hayley had to do now was to keep the tip of the rod up and land the fish, but that's easier said than done.

Hayley smiled to herself as she stepped out of the car.

CHAPTER THIRTEEN

She walked into Johnnie's apartment unable to conceal her exalted sense of accomplishment, which she wore all over her face. Johnnie noticed and commented immediately: "Damn, girl; what got into you? You look like you just had the best sex of your life."

"I did", Hayley answered. "This morning, and you were there. I haven't stopped smiling since."

"Wow, what a sweet talker. I do in fact remember that, and I'm starting to feel like it's time for the matinee", Johnnie said.

"Where's Brendan?" Hayley wanted to know.

"Out somewhere, but even if he were here I wouldn't invite him to join us", Johnnie said, facetiously.

"That's disgusting, Reinhartsen. What? I was a stripper so I must be a whore, too?" Hayley asked defensively.

"I never said that, but it does make you wonder", Johnnie struck back.

Hayley didn't reply. She just turned, tears welling, walked into the bedroom and locked the door. Johnnie was in the mood to hurt Hayley but didn't quite know why. He just had a nagging feeling that something was different, that he was no longer the center of her universe. And he resented it. For Johnnie it was all or nothing. There was no in between.

Hayley emerged half an hour later ready to do battle, but Johnnie had forgotten all about their little spat by then. He was stoned, of course, and very much caught up in an old Brady Bunch re-run on TV. He had a wild crush on Marcia and watched at least two episodes a day – his dirty little secret.

"You and I need to talk, John", Hayley announced.

"Oh, boy; here we go", he immediately thought to himself as the paranoia from that last joint he smoked began to set in. "We're finally up to the part where the beautiful female lead tells the loser leading male that she's done. That she can't imagine how or why she even spent as much time with him as she did." He suspected all along that he was in way over his head, that it was only a matter of time. "Maybe she met some model-looking motherfucker who's into going to the galleries and being part of the 'scene', whatever the fuck *that* was. Well, fuck them both." He was talking to himself outloud in his altered state of consciousness. "When it comes right down to it all I really need is my M&M's – my marijuana and my money. And, let's face it – I'm a pretty good looking guy. A triple threat like me could wander out and be with any female on the planet. Oh, well, all good things must come to an end. At least I still have a brother."

"What is it that's so important you're willing to interrupt my favorite Brady Bunch episode, Hayley?" he wanted to know. "Fucking Davey Jones is just about to sing 'Girl, Look What You've Done to Me' to Marcia at the school dance while all the MILF chaperones cream in their pants without even pretending to hide it. Classic '70's TV porn. Can't it wait another ten minutes?" he asked, feigning cockiness in an effort to show Hayley it didn't matter to him if she wanted to leave.

"No Johnnie, it can't. And you're not necessarily gonna like what I have to say", Hayley warned him.

"Shit, I knew this day was coming", Johnnie blurted out. "I may be a stoner but I'm nobody's fool. Did you meet someone else, or did you just get tired of me?" Johnnie wanted to know.

"Oh, you're somebody's fool alright – MINE", Hayley corrected him. "This isn't about me and you Johnnie, it's about Brendan."

"What *about* Brendan, is he okay?" Johnnie asked with both heightened concern and a sense of relief.

"Well, for the time being I'd say he is, but I think his luck is about to run out", Hayley replied.

"What the fuck is that supposed to mean, Hayley", Johnnie demanded to know.

"Johnnie, remember when you hit the big guy in the face with the bottle at the strip club?" Hayley reminded him.

"Yeah – don't tell me he's dead!" Johnnie panicked.

"No, fortunately he's not, but you certainly could have killed him", Hayley scolded. "Anyway, it turns out that cracking somebody across the face with a bottle for no apparent reason is a felony in NYC. I know this because I had a visit from a detective a week or so ago and he asked all kinds of questions about you."

"I thought this was about Brendan?" Johnnie protested. "Why are we focused on me all of a sudden? What did you tell him?"

"Well, he was really backing me into a corner and scaring me", Hayley admitted. "Kept saying you could be put away for a very long time, and since I obviously knew you I could be put away as an accessory if I didn't give him some useful information."

"What do you mean, 'obviously knew me'?" Johnnie wondered. "He had no fucking idea we knew each other, until you told him – which I'm guessing is the next part of the story."

"I was scared, Johnnie", Hayley went on. "I didn't know what to do. Then it hit me. If I could give him something more valuable to his career than a minor incident at a strip club, maybe he'd leave us both alone."

"Jesus Fucking Christ, Hayley. You gave him Brendan, didn't you??" Johnnie was getting heated. "You filled him in on your little fucking fantasy that Brendan killed my parents." Johnnie could tell from the look on her face that he was right. "What the fuck, Hayley? Why would you do that? Why would you casually end the ten minutes of fucking joy I got to experience for the first time in my miserable life? Are you that heartless? I told you I didn't give a shit either way, that I wanted you to leave it alone. But apparently you didn't give a shit either."

"I'm sorry, John; it was all I had", Hayley shot back. "I couldn't deal with the thought of you going to prison for God knows how long so I had to come up with something fast. Besides, you know I think he did it. I'm afraid of Brendan. I think he's capable of hurting us both, maybe even killing us. He's not what you think he is, Johnnie."

"Bullshit!" Johnnie was seething now. "I'm starting to believe you're not what I think you are, Hayley."

"How could you say that to me, Johnnie?" Hayley wondered. "I've never been anything but straight with you. Please, John; come with me tomorrow and talk to this detective. He wants you to look at some of the crime scene photos to see if anything catches your eye and helps solve the case. Who knows, maybe you'll be able to prove it wasn't Brendan. Please John, come with me tomorrow", Hayley begged.

"This is un-fucking believable", Johnnie uttered. "I'll come, but only to prove you wrong. And when I do, you'd better never bring it up again."

"I won't, John", Hayley swore. I won't."

"And stop calling me 'John'" he implored. "That was my father's name, and I'm not my father."

Hayley was relieved to have that conversation behind her. She'd been a nervous wreck over how Johnnie would react and felt like she was a little bit ahead of the game now; that he didn't freak out nearly as much as she thought he would. Once again she could feel her father's spirit guiding her. "Expect the worst, hope for the best" he would tell her whenever she was about to do something she didn't have a good handle on.

She'd called Dellanno in front of Johnnie and told him he'd see the two of them in the morning. "Does 10 a.m. work for you, detective?" Hayley wanted to know.

"10 a.m. works fine, Ms. Mullany", Dellanno replied. "I'll look forward to seeing you then."

"Thanks Bobby, see you at ten", Hayley said as she hung up the phone.

"'Thanks *Bobby*'?" Johnnie said, jumping all over her. "Who the fuck is Bobby?" Johnnie wanted to know.

"The detective. He told me to call him by his first name, so I did", Hayley said in an attempt to casually brush it aside. But she was completely caught off guard and Johnnie picked up on it.

"And how often do you and *Bobby* get together to plot out how you're gonna fuck my brother for the rest of his life, *Hayley*" Johnnie asked, pulling no punches.

"I met with him once at the precinct, at his request, to talk about what happened at the club", Hayley lied. "And to try and keep *you* out of jail, *Johnnie*. You know what - fuck this. I'm going down to the studio to paint and try and work off some of the anger I'm feeling toward you right now. I don't know what's gotten into you lately, but do us both a favor and tuck the demon back into whatever crevasse he came out of and leave him there. I don't like him."

"Whatever, Hayley", Johnnie replied with an I-don't-really-give-a-shit tone in his voice. "You go down to the studio that I pay for and enjoy yourself. Maybe you can call your friend Bobby and work on how the two of you can really bury Brendan. Prison just doesn't seem like punishment enough for a double-murdering motherfucker like him."

"Fuck you, Johnnie", Hayley said as she stormed out the door. "I didn't know you could be such an asshole."

"Thanks honey, have fun. I'm looking forward to the make-up sex", Johnnie yelled after her. But the second the door closed he knew he'd gone too far. "What the fuck is wrong with me?" he thought as he took another toke and closed his weary eyes.

Hayley decided to play hard ball and sleep on the futon in her studio that night. Johnnie's comment about him paying for the studio really pissed her off. But she was really mad at herself. She went into this whole Johnnie thing eyes wide open despite the fact that she was certain letdown would rear its ugly head at some point. But was this really the deal breaker? Maybe it's just a bump in the road, she thought. Maybe it's time to put the effort into working through pain and disappointment rather than running away from it. In any event, she'd wait to see what Johnnie's demeanor was like in the morning.

It's about time she grew up and learned to trust people. She realized for the first time since her father died that she didn't want her life to end up being nothing more than a series of hit and runs. She needed roots. She needed things to go back to the way they were before Bill Mullany became "Fireman Bill the Hero".

"Please God, help me get through this", Hayley asked the Almighty, as though they had a direct line of communication with each other. "I just can't handle another big letdown."

It's funny how quickly people turn back to 'God' when things get desperate.

Johnnie couldn't fall asleep that night and was beginning to think all the weed in the world wasn't going to help. So he got up, got dressed and went down to Hayley's studio. It was 2:30 in the morning when he rang the bell and yet Hayley managed to get to the door before the ringer's sustain died out. She couldn't fall asleep, either.

"What are you doing here, Johnnie?" she asked.

"Couldn't sleep. I acted like an asshole before and I wanted to apologise", Johnnie informed her.

"Really?" asked Hayley. "That's pretty big of you, Johnnie Boy."

"Does that mean you accept my apology?" Johnnie wondered.

"I suppose so", Hayley replied. "That was our first fight. It was inevitable. I'm just glad it's over with", Hayley let him know.

"Me, too", Johnnie said. "I don't know what the fuck is wrong with me. I guess I'm feeling insecure these days. Truth is I've never had a real relationship before, not even with my own parents, and I don't really know how to act when I'm in one. I hope you have it in you to help me figure it all out", Johnnie fished.

"I don't have it in me *right now*, but I will shortly", Hayley joked. Now, about that make-up sex..."

They awoke in each other's arms at 9:40 a.m.

"Shit!!" Hayley screamed.

"What??" Johnnie screamed even louder. "Is there a spider on me?!?"

"No, we overslept, you little freak", she said. "We're supposed to be at the station house in 20 minutes."

"Oh, man", Johnnie moaned. "Do I really have to go through with this?"

"We had a deal. I'll be the first to admit I was wrong if that turns out to be the case but we'll never know unless we do this", Hayley said with authority. "Now get up and get dressed."

"Yes, sir", Johnnie said with a mock salute. He'd decided as he was falling asleep earlier that he'd try and be more agreeable as a general rule. "Although, it wouldn't hurt to slip up now and then", he quickly thought. "The make-up sex is unbelievable."

When they arrived at the station house Dellanno was waiting for them with 2 hot Starbuck lattes. "I figured you could use these", the detective said. "I know how you youngins like to sleep in. Let's go into the Lieutenants office where it's more comfortable. He's out today and we can use his conference table."

Hayley and Johnnie did as they were instructed and followed Dellanno into the office. As they sat down, Dellanno introduced himself to Johnnie. "I'm Detective Dellanno, Mr. Reinhartsen. But please, call me Bobby", he said.

"Thanks, *detective*", Johnnie replied, refusing to play along. "I'm Johnnie. But please, continue calling me Mr. Reinhartsen."

"Fair enough, *Mr. Reinhartsen*. And how are you today, Ms. Mullany?" Dellanno asked cordially.

"I'm fine, thank you detective", she replied.

"What's with all the formalities, you two?" Johnnie wanted to know. "You're old friends. Feel free to call each other by your given names. I'm sure that's what you do when you're chatting it up on your cell phones." He just couldn't help himself.

"Sorry to get you up so early, Johnnie", Dellanno offered. "It obviously made you very cranky. Let's get

down to business so you can get back home in time for
your morning nappy."

"Jerkoff", Johnnie whispered under his breath.

"Douchebag", Dellanno whispered back. "OK, John.
I'm gonna show you some photos that were taken at the
crime scene the day your parents were murdered. Just a
heads up – they're pretty grizzly so if you need to turn
away that's fine", he continued. "What I'd like you to do
is look closely at every aspect of each photo and let me
know if anything looks strange or out of place to you. Do
you think you could do that, Mr. Reinhartsen?"

"Do I look retarded to you, detective", Johnnie
answered.

"A little bit, but I'm trying not to pass judgement.
They taught us that at the Academy", Dellanno replied,
looking over at Hayley and smiling. "Now this first series
of photos I'm about to show you are of your mother. I
know you're the one who found her, so this will look
familiar to you, but I need you to look at every detail in the
room and see if anything odd jumps out at you."

Johnnie took the photos of his dead mother from
Dellanno's hand and grimaced as he looked through the
stack. He hadn't bothered taking a very close look when
he found her on the bed that day, but seeing close-up for
the first time the horror of what she went through was a
bit much for him. "Well the first thing that 'jumps out at
me' is the fact that Jacquie's brains are no longer inside her
head. That's odd, wouldn't you say, detective?"
antagonized Johnnie.

"Under the circumstances, not really", Dellanno said, as even as could be. "A couple of good smacks with a Louisville Slugger is all you need to achieve this type of result. Keep looking. And do me a favor? Try not to point out the obvious again. You're just eating into your own nap time."

"You didn't specify that in your initial instructions. Thanks for clarifying." Johnnie wasn't going to make this easy for Bobby.

"Anyway, do you see anything that might be useful in determining what actually happened that day?" Dellanno prodded.

"I do not, detective", Johnnie admitted. "Everything looks like it's in place."

Hayley was relieved to see Johnnie getting more serious about the task at hand.

"OK, let's move on then", Dellanno suggested. "I'm gonna show you some pictures of your dad now. As you know, he was found in the garage. Certain pictures I won't present. No one should have to see their loved ones in such a horrifying state."

"He was an asshole, wouldn't bother me either way", Johnnie replied, pretending not to have a care in the world.

"We'll keep those pix in our back pocket for now if it's all the same to you." Dellanno said. "Again, I ask that you take a good look around the garage and see if you notice anything that might be different. That applies to what you can see of your father as well. Here you go."

Johnnie scrutinized the photos of his dead dad without showing any emotion. He was curious about why certain aspects of the photo were blacked out, mainly the areas around his head and neck. He wondered what could be hidden under the black ink that appeared to be suffocating his father in the photo. "Nothing in the garage looks weird, but there is something that's not right with my dad", Johnnie said when he was done. "His Syracuse football ring isn't on his smashed finger. Why are his fingers smashed, anyway", Johnnie wanted to know.

"That's part of the mystery", Dellanno said. "Tell me more about the ring."

"He was Orange through and through. Nothing made him more proud than wearing that ring", Johnnie explained. "He NEVER took it off, not for any reason. He was awarded the game ball when the Orange Men crushed Temple in 1980, his senior year. Proudest moment of his miserable life. That ring was a constant reminder of his 'moment of greatness', as he liked to call it."

"You're sure?" Dellanno asked. "Because this could be a really important piece of the puzzle. Why do you think the only thing missing is that ring? Did he have a rival from Temple who also played in that game? Did he have any rivals in general who might have had a reason to do this and knew the ring was that important to your father?"

"My dad had about a million rivals", Johnnie answered. "He treated everyone like shit his whole life and the more successful he became, the worse he treated people. He was one nasty son-of-a-bitch."

"Well, if that's really true, I can see why you disliked him so much", Dellanno told Johnnie. "Did you ever think about killing him yourself, Johnnie", he asked.

"All the time", Johnnie said without hesitation. "But I guess someone beat me to the punch."

"So give me one good reason to believe I shouldn't be looking at you for the crime", the detective asked in a much more serious tone.

"I'll give you two good reasons", Johnnie told him. "One, I was 16 years old at the time and way too much of a pussy to kill anyone; and two, I loved my mother even though she was a hopeless drunk. Even if I did have the balls to kill Big John, I never would have hurt my mother. So if you're looking at me, you might as well start looking elsewhere and stop wasting both of our time."

Dellanno sat there looking at Johnnie for what seemed like a long time but didn't say a word. He was sizing him up, looking for a 'tell' - an eye twitch, or anything else that might help him decide whether or not to believe him. But Johnnie gave him nothing. Instead, he sat calmly staring right back into the detective's eyes, barely blinking. "OK, well I'll need a good description of that ring. Is there anything else in any of the photos I've shown you that stands out?" Detective Dellanno wanted to know.

"I'd have to say no, Bobby", Johnnie replied. "Can I still call you 'Bobby' or have I lost that privilege?"

"You've done well here today, John", Bobby let him know. "We can start looking to see if that ring ever turned up anywhere. Pawn shops, private collectors, sports memorabilia outlets; places like that. Was there anything unique about the ring? An inscription maybe, or a missing stone?"

"There was an inscription inside the ring. It said 'Big John R-ange'. He was pretty pleased with that, too", Johnnie said. "Came up with it himself, or so he always claimed."

"Good. Well, I guess it's nap time", Dellanno joked. "This was very helpful. Thank you for taking the time to come down here and look at the pictures. That must not have been easy for you."

"I'll be alright. And just for the record, my brother didn't kill anybody, regardless of what my suspicious girlfriend here thinks. I came down here to help you find out some new information. Now you have some ligit places to look. I'm sure Brendan's name isn't gonna appear at the end of any of them so I'd let that go if I were you. Let us know if you come up with anything interesting", Johnnie said as they were leaving.

"Of course. You'll be the first call I make", Dellanno promised.

*

"You see", Hayley said as they were getting into a cab. "That wasn't so bad after all."

"It could've been worse I suppose", Johnnie conceded. "I'm pretty hungry after seeing all those gory death photos of my parents. Why don't we go straight to the diner and get something to eat. By the way, you still think it was Brendan?"

"Until I'm told otherwise", Hayley replied. "But I guess I'm a little less sure now than I was before. That ring thing is kinda weird."

"Well, I hope your buddy proves you wrong quickly. I can't deal with the only two people I care about being at odds with each other like this", Johnnie admitted. "Well, one of you is at odds, anyway; but I still can't deal with it."

"Hopefully it will all be over soon", Hayley reassured him.

CHAPTER FOURTEEN

"This is such fucking bullshit!" Brendan was screaming as he burst into his brother's apartment. "I can't believe they would fucking do this at the last minute. I should've known things were going too smoothly."

"What's the problem, Bren?" Johnnie asked. "You OK?"

"The problem is I have a moving truck coming in about an hour with all my shit from my parent's house and some jerkoff from the board just called me and said I can't move in today because the freight elevator is down and they don't want me to scratch up the passenger elevators", Brendan told Johnnie and Hayley. "What kind of bullshit is that? I'll fucking buy new passenger elevators if they get scratched. I'll buy the whole fucking building for that matter. Assholes."

"Wow, that was some hissy fit you just threw, bro", Johnnie joked. "Relax, we'll figure something out. How long until they get the elevator running again?"

"Probably not for a few days", Johnnie said. "I guess I'll have to put it all in storage until then. I mean, it's not a ton of shit. Mostly clothes and some stuff from my room that I wanted to keep. My aunt and uncle told me after my mom's funeral that they'd deal with selling the house and getting rid of all the other shit. Thank God for them, Bro.

If I had to deal with all this on my own I wouldn't have any idea what to do. Shit would be sitting there for years."

"Why don't you just have them bring your stuff to the studio and leave it there", Hayley suggested. "It's only a couple of flights up. They can use the stairs and then when the elevator is fixed we'll help you move it into your apartment."

"Are you serious? That's an excellent solution, Hayley Girl", Johnnie said, surprised.

"That would work", Brendan chimed in. "Thanks Hayley. Good save."

Johnnie smiled to himself. Maybe all was not lost after all.

The movers got there late and didn't finish unloading the truck until about 9 p.m. After Brendan finished rummaging through the boxes to make sure everything was there, he suggested the three of them go out for a good dinner and lots of alcohol. Johnnie was game but Hayley said she was exhausted and was just going to stay in, take a bath and watch TV. "But you boys go out and have yourselves a good time", she told them. Johnnie didn't know what had gotten into Hayley but maybe their little trip to the 1st Precinct somehow helped to change her mind about Brendan. Whatever the reason, Johnnie felt a sense of relief.

*

Hayley ran the bath in her studio, took off her clothes and lit up a nice sized roach she'd been holding onto. She settled into the tub and took a long, deep toke. Then she picked up her cell phone. She didn't need to open her contact file; at this point she knew the number by heart. After 3 rings he picked up. "You got Dellanno", he said without looking at the caller ID.

"I do?" Hayley asked, suggestively.

"Now that's a loaded question, miss", Dellanno played along.

"Is that anything like a loaded pistol, detective?" Now she was pushing it.

"You have to be especially careful when handling a loaded pistol, Ma'am; it could discharge at any moment without warning. Some of them even have a hair trigger, making them all the more sensitive to the touch." Dellanno advised.

"You'll need to learn to control your weapon if you're ever gonna use it properly, detective." She was getting down to business now. "So listen, I'm in my studio right now with boxes and boxes of Brendan's possessions. It seems the freight elevator is down and the Board won't let him use the passenger elevators to move in so I told him he could store his stuff here until it's fixed. Pretty fucking shrewd of me, no detective?"

"Pretty fucking shrewd of you, yes, Ms. Mullany. I still say you'd make a great cop", Dellanno replied.

"And to top it off, Johnnie and Brendan are out for the night living it up", Hayley went on. "Knowing them, once they get started they won't be home for hours. If I were you I'd get the fuck over here and start looking through his shit for some physical evidence. You'll never get a better opportunity."

"I was just leaving the Station House", he told her. "I can be there in 15 minutes."

"Ok, but I hope I'm not still in the tub when you get here", Hayley said. "That would be pretty embarrassing."

"Well, we wouldn't want to embarrass you now, would we?" Dellanno teased while suddenly remembering what it was like to be 16 again. "See you in 10 minutes."

As she hung up the phone, Hayley shivered against an unlikely thought. "It can't really be this easy, can it? And this guy's a *detective*??" She was starting to feel pretty cocky.

Hayley answered the door with nothing on but a towel, which just barely covered her. "I'm sorry detective, I must have fallen asleep in the tub", she lied. "Just give me a sec while I get some clothes on."

"Please, take your time", Dellanno replied. "Personally, I find clothes are not all they're cracked up to be."

"Then you won't mind if I just keep the towel on", Hayley suggested. "I like to let my body air dry. It's better for the pores."

"Whatever makes you comfortable", Dellanno said.

Hayley let the towel slip to the floor. "Oops! How clumsy of me!" Hayley teased, looking Dellanno directly in the eye as she moved in for the kill. "So, are we gonna continue to ignore the fact that there's a python in the room and just keep dancing around it, or are we gonna do something about it?"

Before she even finished the sentence Dellanno was on her. As they kissed he pushed her down onto the futon. She didn't put up a fight. This time there was no uncomfortable steering wheel in the way and no nosey passers-by. It was just the two of them. And they made the most of their time alone together.

As they lay on the futon, sweaty and satisfied, Dellanno thought to himself "am I out of my fucking mind?! I could lose my badge over something like this." He looked over at Hayley, who was lighting up what was left of the roach, and said "time to get a look at what's in those boxes. Can you pass me my clothes?"

"Is the little detective feeling shy all of a sudden?" she teased.

"Not at all, I just don't want you to be tempted when we've got work to do", he replied. "If I stand here all bare-assed naked, there's no way you're going to be able to keep your hands off of me."

"You're probably right", she said. "Here, take a hit of this and then we'll get to work."

"No thanks miss. I've already violated about a dozen cop rules, and probably a few of Mother Nature's as well in the last half hour", Dellanno admitted. "Let's just see if we can find something that supports your theory about McAvoy."

"All work and no play", Hayley said.

"I'll make you a deal – if we find anything interesting, I'll play with you all you want later on", he promised.

"That sounds reasonable", said Hayley.

Johnnie and Brendan decided they needed to consume several slabs of meat for dinner and ended up on the east side at BLT Prime in Gramercy. Brendan picked the venue not only for the prime aged beef, but also because he liked Molly Malone's Pub, which was right around the corner on 3rd Avenue. It reminded him of the Pubs he'd been to in Ireland as a young boy with Tom and Laura when they'd visit Tom's family every summer. Their plan was to head to Molly's after dinner and drink Guinness until they could drink no more. They were both in the mood to get hammered. The two were getting along exceptionally well by now and were unambiguously enjoying each other's company. Brendan could always feel Tom and Laura's presence whenever he stepped foot inside an Irish Pub and this evening was no different. That's when the magnitude of recent events came crashing down on him.

"What's up, Brendan?" Johnnie asked, immediately sensing Brendan's change in demeanor.

"I don't know", Brendan answered. "It's like I'm realizing for the first time that my parents are dead. It all happened so quickly I guess it never really sank in. My parents are dead, John. I'm an orphan now."

"Welcome to the club", Johnnie said. "You get used to it after a while. It becomes normal, just like everything else. If you give anything enough time it'll get inside your system and make you feel like it's been there all along."

"I suppose", Brendan acknowledged. "Still sucks at the moment, however."

"Hang in there, bro", Johnnie encouraged his brother. "We still got each other."

"You know, I was thinking", Brendan went on. "We've got all this money and property all over the place. We should do something with it. Something substantial. Tom used to tell me all the time never to forget to give back and help the less fortunate. We should do that."

"Do what?" Johnnie was confused.

"Give back." Brendan reiterated.

"Give back to who?" asked Johnnie.

"To the less fortunate, you fucking idiot. You know you really need to cut back on your weed consumption.

Talking to you is like talking to a plant sometimes", Brendan informed him.

"Fuck you, bro", Johnnie snapped back. "Who is it you're planning on helping, anyway?"

"Well, I was thinking", Brendan continued. "Since I've been living in the city I've noticed there's an unbearable amount of homeless people around. Here I am living in my brother's luxurious Central Park apartment and there are people right across the street with nothing but the ratty clothes on their backs. They're filthy, they're hungry, they're cold and they're alone. They have no idea where their next meal is coming from and they have nothing to look forward to. Just doesn't seem right. With all the money we have we should be able to help at least some of them, no?

"I mean, *technically*, yeah. Should be a no-brainer", Johnnie agreed. "But where do you even start?"

"Well, I've actually been giving that a lot of thought, too", Brendan said, not missing a beat. "First thing we'd need to do is buy an old warehouse and gut it. There are plenty around. Once we've got that, we buy a shit load of those old cargo containers you see on those giant freighters – you know, the ones you can stack one on top of the other. Then we outfit them with some drywall, electricity, heat, A/C, a bathroom with a shower, a small kitchen and some bunk beds. Stack 'em 3 high and fill the warehouse with 'em. Instant homes for the homeless. You can get four people in each easily. We'll call it Rein-Mac Housing."

"Nice idea", Johnnie agreed. "But all that would cost a fortune. And how many people can you build homes for? A few hundred, a thousand maybe? And there must be all kinds of regulations and approvals we'd need to deal with." Johnnie was playing devil's advocate. "And, what's that gonna do for the overall homeless population?"

"I'm not suggesting we're gonna solve the homeless problem on our own, but it would be a good start", Brendan said. "If we can show it works, we can go out and get investors, raise a shitload of money and help thousands and thousands more people. Get the power companies to donate electricity. Give them clean cloths and bring in people who can teach them how to be a part of society again, help them find work and get back on their own two feet."

"You think you're gonna put 3 or 4 people who have been living on the street for God knows how long into a fucking *container* together and they're *not* gonna kill each other?" Johnnie was wondering.

"We implement a zero tolerance rule", Brendan retorted. "First sign of trouble and you're out. Period. If people want to have shelter, sleep in a bed, shower and eat regular meals for the simple price of tolerating one another, they'll adapt. It's known as classical conditioning."

"And who's gonna invest money in something like that?" Johnnie wanted to know.

"Are you fucking kidding me?" Brendan said. "What company or foundation in their right mind *wouldn't* contribute to help house the homeless? It's like the fucking Holy Grail of philanthropy in New York City. That's a good name for the project, by the way: "Help House the Homeless". If a couple of 18 year olds are willing to put their own money where their mouths are, major corporations and foundations will look pretty fucking bad not following suit. Tom and Laura's estate is worth $20+ million dollars. You and I both have enough money already for the next 5 generations of our families to live on without even counting that twenty. I'm willing to put up my mother and father's entire estate to make this work. Whaddaya think? "Rein-Mac Corporation: Housing the Homeless". We partner-up and do something good for society. It would go a long way in cleaning up all the bad karma our parents created. This will work, Bro. I'm telling you."

"Pretty ambitious, dude. And crazy, but I'm not saying no. Let me think about it. It's a nice gesture but I'm a lazy, pot smoking slacker. You sure you'd want me as your partner for something so important?" Johnnie asked.

"John – either your my brother or you're not. I'd like to continue thinking you are. And I'd love to have you in the family business. Whaddaya say, Bro?"

"I say let me sleep on it. Cool?" Johnnie wanted to know.

"Cool", Brendan assured him.

*

Hayley sat on the futon and watched as Dellanno methodically went through each of Brendan's boxes. He was careful not to disturb anything but was determined to leave no stone unturned. Most of the boxes contained clothes. Several held sporting goods and a few were jam-packed with Brendan's trophies, which he could never bring himself to part with; not even his T-Ball trophy. His name wasn't even on that one, just the year and the name of the league. But that didn't matter to Brendan. He remembered the coach putting it in his hand and high-fiving him as if it had happened yesterday. For him it held the same significance as the Varsity baseball MVP trophy he'd received only a few months ago. Then Dellanno found a box containing some personal items: letters, photos, CD's, condoms, rolling papers and a small jewellery box. He was wearing gloves so he wouldn't leave his prints on anything, just in case, and didn't hesitate to pick up the box and look inside. There was the usual array of teenage adornment: puka shell necklaces, Jesus and St. Joseph miraculous medals, ID bracelets and assorted watches and rings. As he was sorting through the items in the box he noticed one of the rings was different than the others. He picked it up and knew immediately what he was holding. It was Big John's Syracuse football ring with the inscription "Big John R-ange" on the inside.

"HO-LEE-FUCK!" Dellanno blurted out. "I can't believe it. This is it. This is what we've been looking for!"

"What's what we've been looking for?" Hayley wanted to know. "What did you find, Bobby?"

"This is fucking incredible. You were right, Hayley. That son-of-a-bitch did do it." Dellanno exclaimed. "It's literally the only thing that could have tied him to the crime and the cocky bastard had the balls to keep it in his possession."

"Keep *what* in his possession? What the fuck are you talking about, Bobby?" Hayley demanded to know.

"Have a look", Dellanno said, holding up the evidence. "It's Big John's Syracuse ring. No doubt about it. The inscription is right here." He showed the ring to Hayley without letting her touch it.

"Jesus Christ! I knew it!!" Hayley screamed. "I knew that fucker did it! No one wanted to believe me. You gotta pick him up right away, Bobby. You gotta! He's fucking dangerous and he's gonna wind up hurting me and Johnnie at some point." Hayley was freaking out now.

"Slow down, Hayley", Bobby said. "I need time to think this through so there are no holes. I didn't exactly follow proper police procedure here. If that gets out the evidence will be inadmissible in court. Let me sit on this for a day or two. At the very least we need to say the box was sitting there open, in plain view. We need to come up with a good reason for my being here as well. I'm gonna take the ring with me. Leave the box sitting where it is. Do your best to keep Brendan out of the studio until I can figure out the optimal approach. Can you do that, Hayley?"

"I don't know", Hayley answered nervously. "What if he starts to figure things out and comes after me? What do I do then, Bobby? I don't like this. I'm scared."

"He's not gonna figure anything out", Dellanno assured her. "He's already looked through the boxes and presumably taken what he needed. And he won't remember whether or not he took the jewellery box out and left it sitting there. This is big, Hayley. Stay upstairs in Johnnie's place and you'll be fine. Trust me."

"Ok Bobby, but don't drag this out too long. Please", Hayley begged.

"I won't. I promise", Bobby told her.

Hayley had gone back up to Johnnie's apartment while he and Brendan were out and was asleep by the time they got home. They walked in at 4:30 am with bacon, egg and cheese sandwiches from the 24 hour deli down the street. They were loud and obnoxious as they ate but they were also in an unusually good mood. Hayley could tell by the way they joked and laughed as they wolfed down their sandwiches that their relationship had been taken to a new level. This worried her. She knew that what was about to go down with Brendan would devastate Johnnie. She was hoping to get him to see that Brendan was not what he was pretending to be but she'd already lost that battle. She was going to have to figure out how to bring

Johnnie back to a good place after the shit hits the fan. But that wasn't going to be easy. It would either draw him closer to her or it would push him away. Far away. She put the odds at about 50-50. She knew Johnnie well enough to know that it would be one extreme or the other. There was no in between.

The boys smoked one last joint together and decided it was time to go to bed. They gave each other a bro-hug and disappeared into separate bedrooms. Johnnie woke up Hayley, who was only pretending to be asleep, for no reason other than to tell her what a great time he and Brendan had that night. "You're so wrong about him, Hayley Girl", he said. "I wish you'd just get over it and accept the fact that my brother's a good guy. It would make things so much easier all around. I mean, he's not going anywhere anytime soon."

"I can't believe he just said that", Hayley thought to herself. "Fuck! This is gonna be brutal."

CHAPTER FIFTEEN

Brendan sauntered into the living room about 11:30 am looking miserable. Johnnie was already up. The two reeked of stale beer and bar sweat. Hayley was doing her best to swallow down some yogurt and granola but it was rough. She'd been barely managing her way through Johnnie's stench but once Brendan contributed it was all over. Yogurt, granola, stale beer and bar sweat were a horrific combination, she'd decided.

"So I just got a call from that idiot from the board", Brendan announced. "The freight elevator is up and running and he said I could move my stuff in from 2:00 to 4:00 this afternoon. You guys up for a little physical activity later?"

"Sure", said Hayley. "That was the deal. Johnnie should be somewhat human by then, isn't that right, Johnnie Boy?"

"Oh, yeah. Looking forward to it", Johnnie answered in a very non-committal way.

"You guys don't have to worry about it", Brendan said, feeling bad. "The building has hand trucks and valet carts they said I could use. I'll get it done."

"Here's an even better idea", Johnnie offered. "Why don't you call down and ask Victor and Roberto to do it. Throw them a hundred bucks each and they'll get it done on their lunch break. Works for you and works for them."

"That's fucking brilliant", Brendan said with pure joy in his voice. "See what I mean? This just goes to show, ours will be a very successful business partnership."

"What do you mean 'business partnership'", Hayley asked.

"'Rein-Mac Corporation: Housing the Homeless'", Johnnie informed her. "We've decided, based on an idea Brendan had, that it's time to do something productive with a portion of our wealth that benefits society. We're going to use the McAvoy estate to fund a business that builds shelters, little apartments actually, for homeless people."

"So does that mean you're in", Brendan asked?

"I'm in", Johnnie replied. "I've been thinking about it a lot and decided you were right, Brendan. It's time I get involved in something useful for once in my miserable fucking existence. It's time to be a productive member of society."

"Well that's very noble of you both, but do either of you know the first thing about building shelters or running a business for that matter?" Hayley wanted to know. "Seems to me if it were that easy it would have been done a long time ago."

"All we need is the capital and the desire, the rest is all for hire", Johnnie said. "Damn, that's good. We're gonna have to use that in our pitch to investors. Anyway, if we can show it can be done successfully on a smaller scale we'll be able to raise the funds to do it on a much larger one. We've got it all figured out."

"That sounds great', Hayley said. "I hope you can pull it off. It would be very gratifying to help so many people get off the street and start to pull their lives together."

Of course what Hayley was really thinking was "Fuck! This is getting more and more complicated by the minute." She hadn't counted on the brothers forging such a tight bond so quickly. "Johnnie's never gonna forgive me for what's about to happen."

Bobby Dellanno couldn't stop thinking about the ring. Most detectives spend their entire career dreaming about finding that one piece of physical evidence that directly links an individual to a crime, particularly a murder case, but it rarely ever happens. This was a once in a lifetime event for him. As he sat drinking his coffee he thought about how to position things so there would be no doubts about him following proper police procedure. He hadn't, of course, but unless he did his best to make it look that way Brendan was going to walk and Hayley was going to be in danger. Brendan surely wouldn't let her get away with what she did, Bobby was certain of that. Once he was satisfied he had solid plan he'd move in and pick Brendan up. But first he had a phone call to make.

"Detective Freedman, how can I help you?" the voice at the other end of the line said.

"Freedman, its Dellanno. I've got some good news for you", Bobby said.

"Talk to me Bobby, whaddaya got?" Freedman wanted to know.

"Oh, I got, detective. I got", Bobby replied.

"Well, do you wanna stop acting like a little school girl about it and share?" Freedman wondered.

"Ok, I'll give you that one", Bobby conceded. "What I've got is a ring with Big John Reinhartsen's inscription inside that could only have been taken by whoever took the Louisville Slugger to the back of his head."

"And how, pray tell, did you manage to come across such a damning piece of evidence, detective?" Freedman asked, sceptically. "How in the hell did you even know that such a piece of evidence existed?" Freedman wanted to know.

"Well, remember I told you about the female I was working with on that other case – the one that was willing to give me this if I let her and her boyfriend skate on a minor incident at a strip club?" Bobby said, more as a reminder than a question.

"Yeah, yeah; I remember. She'd only talk to you. Go on", Freedman said, somewhat impatiently.

"What I *didn't* tell you was that her boyfriend is John Reinhartsen, Jr., the victims' son", Bobby informed him. "And the kid I'm looking at, excuse me – the kid 'we' are looking at - is his half-brother, Brendan McAvoy, the illegitimate son of Big John Reinhartsen."

"Fuck me", Freedman said with genuine surprise in his voice. "But you still didn't explain about the ring."

"I had Jr. look at some of the crime scene photos to see if he noticed anything that was out of place - something your boy Mazzetti never did, by the way - and the first thing he saw was that the ring was missing from his father's smashed-up finger. He noticed it because Big John apparently never took the thing off, he was so proud of it. I held back the more gory photos though, especially the one with the bike pump", Dellanno explained.

"I'm with you", Freedman advised. "Please continue."

"It was obvious at that point that since all his other jewellery was still on his person, as were his very expensive watch, his cash and his credit cards, that this was not a random home invasion or a burglary. This was Murder One and whoever the killer was, he had Reinhartsen's ring. Probably took it as a souvenir – standard fair for depraved murdering sonsofbitches, as you know", Bobby went on.

"So how did this young lady get involved with the victim's kid?" Freedman wanted to know.

"Ran into him in Central Park one morning, totally by chance", Bobby said. "They smoked some weed together and wound up hooking up."

"And you came across this ring *how?*" Freedman pressed.

"I'm glad you asked, detective. It was very fortuitous, actually", Bobby explained. "Brendan bought an apartment in his brother's building after Jr. ponied up half his inheritance after some DNA testing confirmed the relationship. When he went to move in he couldn't because the freight car was down. So he wound up storing his shit in the girls studio apartment downstairs in the same building. When the brothers were out partying one night, the girl called me at the House and told me what the situation was. I went over and there in plain sight was this kid Brendan's jewellery box with the ring sitting in it."

"How fortuitous, indeed" Freedman said. "I buy everything but the part about the ring being 'in plain sight'. You're full of shit, detective; and you know it."

"You want to share credit for solving this monumental murder mystery or you want to poke holes in my story?" Dellanno wanted to know. "Look, as far as we're both concerned, this is how it went down. In fact, you were there with me, we went in together and there it was."

"Probably makes sense to tell it that way", Freedman admitted. "OK, let's go with it."

"Good", Bobby said. "I called you after receiving a call from the girl saying she had the proof we needed to grab this kid Brendan. When we got there the box and the ring were in plain sight. We can say the kid had taken it out of the storage box on his own and left the jewellery box open. We'll fine tune the details and sink up the rest of the story later."

"I can live with that", Freedman admitted. "Sometimes you have to sacrifice your own integrity for the greater good. Getting this kid off the street so he can't hurt anyone else is the right thing to do, regardless of whether or not we have to bend some bullshit rules to make it happen."

"I couldn't agree more, detective", Bobby said. "It would make sense for you to be there with me when we grab this kid up. I'll swear we worked the case together the whole time."

"Just give me the word, Bobby", Freedman said. "I'll be there."

Bobby got home that night exhausted. He took a quick shower and climbed into bed. He was careful not to wake his wife, Gina. He still had a lot of thinking to do and he didn't want to get into a long conversation about why he missed yet another little league game. His son, Christopher, was used to him being a no-show at this point and didn't take it personally, but Bobby knew that didn't make it right. He vowed to himself and to his sleeping wife that when this was all over he was going to be a more attentive father. Just as soon as he figured out what he was going to do about Hayley. "What a fucking idiot I am", he thought to himself as he drifted off to sleep.

Brendan had arranged for his furniture delivery to come late on the day he was originally scheduled to move in. He called Restoration Hardware and Pottery Barn, explained his dilemma, and they were only too happy to accommodate him. "Call us a few hours before you want it and we'll get it there immediately", both store managers informed him. They remembered that Brendan walked into their stores and spent money like he had an unlimited supply of it, so they immediately put him at the top of their "preferred customer" lists, which grants the consumer royalty treatment the moment he or she calls or walks through the door again. The average person never sees this kind of treatment because the average person doesn't possess an unlimited supply of cash. Guaranteeing customer loyalty and repeat business from the big spenders is the name of the game and retail merchants are the grand masters. No one understands the psychology of human behavior better. Sigmund Freud would have done well to spend some time observing the masters at work.

As he sat on the window sill in his new living room staring vacantly at the park below, his thoughts having fallen upon the myriad of homeless people he was going to save as he waited for his take-out to arrive, Brendan was startled by a loud knock on the door. It was more of a loud pounding, actually.

"Hold on", he screamed. "Jesus Christ", he mumbled under his breath. "Could you delivery guys be any less fucking patient?"

When he opened the door he was surprised to find two gentlemen in suits standing there with four uniformed police officers behind them, each with his hand resting wantonly on the handle of his 9 millimetre automatic.

"You guys clearly aren't delivering food", Brendan said. "I'm thinking you knocked on the wrong door. If you'll excuse me...."

"Brendan McAvoy?" Dellanno asked.

"Who's asking?" Brendan wanted to know.

"I'm Detective Dellanno, NYPD; and this is my colleague, Detective Freedman from the Greenwich Police Department", Dellanno went on. "Mind if we come in?"

"I might. What is it you guys want?" Brendan asked with mounting concern. "Is someone *else* in my family dead? And why do your friends back there look like they're itching to shoot me? What the fuck is going on? I'm very confused."

"I think we can clear it all up for you if you'll allow us to come in. Please?" Dellanno asked in a very professional cop tone.

"I guess", Brendan answered in an exasperated voice.

"Mr. McAvoy, I'd ask that you keep your hands where we can see them at all times. I'm also going to ask that you not move suddenly or attempt to exit the apartment without our permission", Dellanno warned, more than asked. "Perhaps you can have a seat near that window and answer some questions now."

"Ok, this is getting seriously weird", Brendan informed the men. "How do I know you're really cops, anyway? You have some kind of cop ID or anything like that? And I don't like the way your fucking friends over there are looking at me."

"Calm down, Mr. McAvoy", Freedman warned. "If you think they're looking at you funny now, see what happens if you start to act up."

"Easy everybody", Dellanno jumped in. "No one's going to act up. Now Brendan, please give us the courtesy of answering a few of our questions. And you four; why don't you wait out in the hall? If we need you we'll call for you."

The uniforms begrudgingly did as they were asked and Brendan settled down.

"This is my official NYPD identification card. As you can see it has my picture and my shield number, which matches my shield. It's signed by me and by the Commissioner of the New York City Police Department. Does that help put your mind at ease, Brendan?"

"Is this about me smoking weed in the park?" Brendan tried to understand. "'Cause this sure seems like overkill for a little joint or two. Would it help if I promise never to smoke pot again?"

"I'm afraid this is just a tad more serious than smoking a joint in the park, son", Dellanno corrected him.

"Aren't I supposed to get one phone call or something? And aren't you guys supposed to have a search warrant?" Brendan was starting to panic a little now.

"I think you've been watching way too many cop shows on TV", Dellanno surmised. "We haven't arrested you and we didn't force entry - you opened the door and let us in. So, no need for a phone call, and no need for a search warrant. All we want to do is ask you a few questions. Are you ok with that, Brendan?"

"I suppose", Brendan whined. "What is it you need to know? OH! Wait a second – this is about that assault at the strip club, isn't it? Well, I can explain….."

"PLEASE, Mr. McAvoy", Dellanno was running out of patience. "This would work a lot better if you'd just let us ask some questions rather than try and guess what it is we want to know."

"Alright", Brendan conceded. "Ask."

"For a while I thought it was me", Johnnie explained. "But it's not me, Hayley. It's so obviously you. What the fuck is going on? There's a gap the size of Central Park between us and I can't figure out how to get across it."

"I don't know what you're talking about, Johnnie", she replied. "I don't know what you want me to say. You're behaving like a paranoid little boy. Nothing has changed between us. Can we please stop now? I can't do this anymore. I'm fucking exhausted."

"What, are you worried if we split up you won't have a way to support yourself?" Johnnie was relentless. "Because we had an agreement – if the living together thing didn't work out I'd continue to support you until you got back on your feet. If that's the thing that's keeping you here don't do me any fucking favors. I'll hand you a blank check right now."

"Johnnie, Johnnie, Johnnie; YOU'RE the thing that's keeping me here. I don't care about your money, I care about YOU", Hayley did her best to convince him. "Now can we please put this to rest once and for all?"

"Whatever", Johnnie gave in. "Maybe you could use a little space; some time to yourself. Why don't you spend the next few nights on your futon? Maybe that will help you see things more clearly."

"You know what? That's probably a good idea, John", Hayley conceded. "Maybe it will do us both some good. I'll see you later."

She walked over, gave him a kiss on the cheek and made her exit. Johnnie stood there for a few moments taking it all in. In his mind, the fact that she was willing to leave like that validated what he was feeling. Something was up. He just didn't know what.

"Do you know John Reinhartsen Sr. and his wife, Jacqueline, Mr. McAvoy?" Dellanno asked.

"I *knew* them", Brendan replied. "They're both dead now. Why the fuck are you asking me about the Reinhartsen's?"

"How well did you know them?" Dellanno went on, ignoring Brendan's very reasonable question.

"Pretty well", Brendan said. "My father worked for Big John for years and our families used to get together regularly when I was a kid. Why the fuck are you asking me about the Reinhartsen's?"

"And what's your relationship with John Jr., Big John's son?" Dellanno wanted to know.

"I'll make you a deal – you tell me why the fuck you're asking me about the Reinhartsen's two years after they died and I'll answer some more of your questions." Brendan offered.

"John Jr. is your brother, or should I say 'half' brother; isn't that right, Brendan?" Dellanno continued.

Brendan didn't answer. He just sat there with a smug look and engaged in a staring contest with the detective, determined not to be the first to blink or look away.

"Are you aware that Big John was having an affair with your mother, Laura, and that your birth was a direct result of that liaison, Mr. McAvoy?" Dellanno jabbed.

"Are you aware that you're a giant fucking douchebag, Mr. Detective?" Brendan countered.

"I *have* been told that on more than one occasion, as a matter of fact", Dellanno admitted. "But that still doesn't answer my question."

Brendan said nothing.

"Ok, here's the deal: we - 'we' being myself and Detective Freedman here - recently came upon some new evidence relating to the Reinhartsen murders and we're tracking down all those who were close to the family at that time to see if we can garner any additional leads from them. As I'm sure you're aware, the deaths were ruled the result of a random home invasion, but we don't buy that for a second, do we Detective Freedman?"

"We most certainly do not, Detective Dellanno", Freedman agreed. "As a matter of fact we're quite certain it was premeditated murder."

The detectives were leaning in with a little more weight now as they attempted to solicit some kind of reaction from Brendan.

"So what's this got to do with me?" Brendan asked, nervously.

"We're not saying it has anything to do with you, Brendan", Bobby informed him in a calm, friendly voice. "We're just trying to gather information after which we'll see if any of the new bits and pieces fit into the old puzzle. As far as we're concerned there's a killer out there and we'd like to pull him in before someone else ends up dead. It's pretty straight forward."

"So why the need for all the cop muscle if all you want is to ask me a few questions?" Brendan wondered.

"That's a fair question, kid", Dellanno replied. "Standard police procedure dictates that anybody that could be *considered* a potential suspect be approached in this manner. It doesn't mean you *are* a suspect. Now, can you help us, Brendan?"

"I can try, but all I know is what I read in the papers and watched on the news", Brendan told the detectives. "You guys probably know a lot more than me."

"Well, there's a very good chance we do, Brendan", Dellanno agreed. "But, you never know. There might be something no bigger than your little finger that gets uncovered and solves the whole case. It's a tedious process, but there's no better way to unravel the mystery of what actually happened in a cold case like this."

"Why the sudden interest after 2 years." Brendan asked.

"As I said, some new evidence came to light and we're obliged, especially since it was a particularly brutal double homicide, to follow up on it to see if it helps us in any way", Dellanno explained. "If the killer was capable of doing this once, there's nothing to stop him from doing it again, especially if he thinks he got away with it. We'd like to lock him up before he does. Now, what we'd ask is for you to come down to the precinct with us to look at some of the crime scene photos that were taken on the day of the murders. There's a chance, however small, that you may see something that stands out as being odd to you; something that just might help us bring about justice. Can we count on your cooperation, Mr. McAvoy?"

"Well, I guess so", Brendan said with a hint of hesitation in his voice. "But can we maybe do this tomorrow? I've got a shitload of unpacking to do, as you can see, and I'd like to get to it. I'm really anal when it comes to mess."

"We'd actually prefer you came with us right now if you don't mind", Dellanno said. "Det. Freedman needs to get back to Connecticut this evening due to a previous obligation and it's important that he be a part of the process. I'm sure you'll have plenty of opportunities to be 'anal' later on".

"Are you arresting me?" Brendan wanted to know.

"Should we be, Brendan?" Dellanno asked matter-of-factly. "As far as I can tell we're asking you to help us potentially solve a murder because you're closely tied to the victims and might be able to shed some new light on a horribly tragic event."

"I'll do the best I can", Brendan said as they passed the delivery guy in the hall without even acknowledging his presence.

Hayley was glad to be away from Johnnie for a little while. She knew things were going to get ugly as soon as Bobby made his move. She hoped she'd have enough time to come up with a reasonable plan for talking Johnnie off the ledge when he found out.

Johnnie had a sense that she was up to something. And his mind kept going to that cop, *Bobby*. He didn't like that they were so buddy-buddy with each other. The only way a guy and a girl get that friendly that fast is when they're fucking, he thought. But why? Why would she suddenly start fucking around with this guy when he'd been so good to her? He would do anything for her and she knew it. Brendan was right, he thought. Women get bored with guys that are too agreeable, too *nice*. They start to look at them as though they're nothing but pussies. They start to walk all over them. Well, maybe he'd stop being so accommodating. Maybe it was time to get selfish on her. This is why he'd always avoided real relationships in the past. They're just too much work and Johnnie was too lazy to put in that much effort. Maybe it was best they went their separate ways. He'd miss her for sure, but if he could get over his parent's murder, he'd get over this.

CHAPTER SIXTEEN

Dellanno and Freedman walked into the interrogation room about an hour after they first sat Brendan down, and Brendan was furious. "What the fuck! Why did you rush me down here if you were gonna make me sit in this fucking room by myself for an hour???"

"Sorry about that kid", Dellanno replied without emotion. "We had a bit of an emergency to deal with. Didn't mean to keep you waiting." Of course they did mean to keep him waiting and it had Brendan rattled.

"Am I free to leave, because this is bullshit", Brendan protested. "If you need me to look at some pictures you'd better break them out quick or I'm gone. Unless you're arresting me for some major bullshit reason."

"There you go again with that 'arrest' stuff", Dellanno said. "You're starting to sound a lot like someone who did something wrong and expects to get caught. Did you do something wrong, Brendan? Is your conscience bothering you for some reason?"

"The only thing I did wrong was agree to come down here with you in the first place", Brendan told the detective. "Why don't you tell me what's really going on and stop wasting my time?"

"How 'bout we look at those pictures and we'll take it from there", Dellanno suggested.

"If that's what it takes", Brendan agreed.

*

Hayley decided to give Bobby a call on his cell to see if he had a plan yet for picking up Brendan. She wanted to make sure they were in sync. What she really needed to know was the timing, the details were unimportant.

Bobby felt his phone vibrate and looked to see who it was. "Can you guys excuse me for a minute, I need to grab this", he said. He stepped out into the hall and picked up. "Hey, you kinda caught me at a bad time. I've got Brendan in the interrogation room and we're just starting to work on him."

"You already picked him up??" Hayley said anxiously.

"You sound upset", Bobby said, confused. "I'd have thought you'd be happy with that news. Aren't you the one that said 'pick him up as soon as possible'?"

"I did, but I didn't think it was going to be this fast", Hayley admitted. "Do you know if he called Johnnie to tell him?"

"He hasn't called anyone since he's been in our presence", Bobby informed her. "I'll keep him from making the call for a while but I'm only talking an hour, tops. As soon as we hit him with the evidence he's gonna want to lawyer up, at which point he'll probably get in touch with his brother as well."

"Ok, try and buy me as much time as you can", Hayley requested. "And Bobby – thanks."

"Just doing my job, Ma'am", he said with a smile. She couldn't see it, but she could certainly hear it in his voice.

Johnnie was feeling miserable. He'd smoked himself into a stupor and was now thoroughly depressed. He wasn't going to make it through the night with what happened between him and Hayley weighing heavily upon his sluggish mind so he got off the couch and went down to the studio to try and patch things up. He got to her door just in time to hear the end of her conversation with Bobby: "try and buy me as much time as you can. And Bobby – thanks."

"Buy time for what?" Johnnie wondered. "And what are the chances I randomly came to her door and she just happened to be on the phone flirting with that cop? One in a fucking billion? She must be on the phone with that motherfucker *constantly*. She's definitely fucking him. Godfuckingdammit."

He didn't bother going in. He was pretty certain about where their relationship stood at that point. "Oh well, easy come easy go", he tried to tell himself, but even he wasn't buying it. "At least I've still got a brother. Beats being alone again", he said out loud, taking some small measure of comfort from the thought.

*

Dellanno walked back into the room with a manila folder under his arm and a bagged-up, wooden baseball bat in his hand, setting both down on the table without saying a word. He sat there staring at Brendan for a minute and then started to speak. Brendan was visibly disturbed by the detectives play acting.

"Do you know what these are, Brendan?" Dellanno asked.

"Yeah, I know what they are", Brendan replied.

"Do you want to tell me what they are?" Dellanno inquired.

"Well, at the risk of stating the obvious, it looks like you just put an old baseball bat and a big envelope filled with God knows what on the table", Brendan said. "Am I correct, detective?"

"As a matter of fact, you are", Dellanno replied in a good natured way. "That's very observant of you. Can you tell me anything else about these objects, something that might not be so obvious, Brendan?" ("Wow", Dellanno thought. "This kid's as sarcastic as his brother. They definitely share the same DNA.")

"The only other thing I can say is that there's some funky, dried-up shit covering the fat part of the bat", Brendan offered up. "And I'm guessing that that envelope has those crime scene photos you were talking about in them."

"Well that's a good guess, son." Dellanno was obviously patronizing Brendan. "That's exactly what's in that envelope and in a minute we're going to take a careful look at each and every one of them. But first, what do you think that 'dried-up, funky shit' covering the fat part of the bat is, Brendan? Hey, aren't you going to college on a baseball scholarship?"

Brendan ignored the comment about the scholarship. "Looks like it could be some infield dirt, officer", Brendan answered with a patronizing tone of his own. "Maybe some of that expensive red clay like they use in the Bigs. Did you get Derek Jeter to autograph a bat for you and now you want to show it off, detective?".

"Reasonable guess, kid" Dellanno admitted. "But it's the wrong answer. And, no; it's not an autographed Jeter bat. But do you want to know what all that dried-up, funky shit actually is, Brendan?"

"Hit me, Dellanno", Brendan replied. "I'm ready."

"Ok. What you're looking at here, Brendan, is the dried up grey matter of Jacqueline Reinhartsen; you're biological step-mother, in a manner of speaking. You're looking at pieces of her brain, Brendan. Hey, you must have a pretty good swing if you got a full ride to Georgetown, ha kid?"

"How is it you know all this about my private life and my relationship with the Reinhartsen's, detective?" Brendan asked in all sincerity, once again ignoring the baseball references. "As far as I know, there were only a handful of people that had that information about me, Big

John and my mother. I didn't find out myself until two years ago. Johnnie only found out recently because I told him. I only found out because my mother told me. My father, Tom McAvoy, knew it as well. But how did you know, detective? How did you uncover such a big family secret on your own?"

"Ahh, a good detective never gives up his sources, Bren. But it does have a lot to do with that pain staking investigatory process I was telling you about earlier, kid", Dellanno said.

"Stop calling me 'Bren' and 'kid', like we're buddies", Brendan warned. "And if you want my continued cooperation, stop talking to me like I'm an asshole."

"I'm sorry if I came off that way, Brendan. I'll try and be more mindful of that as we proceed with our little show and tell", Dellanno promised. "Now, let's get to those photos, shall we?"

"You're the one taking your sweet fucking time about it, detective", Brendan said. "Is that part of your interrogation strategy, or are you just a little slow to begin with?"

"Touché, Mr. McAvoy", Dellanno complimented. "You're pretty quick on your feet. I hope I can keep up."

"I'll try not to get too far ahead of you", Brendan replied with plenty of sarcasm.

Dellanno took his time opening the envelope and laying the photos out in front of Brendan one at a time.

"This first one here, this is how your brother found your step-mom when he walked into the bedroom the day she was murdered", Dellanno informed Brendan. "As you can see, someone took that bat we found lying next to her and cracked her skull wide open with it before placing it gently by her side. The bat in that photo is the same bat you see sitting here on the table in front of you; the one with your step-moms brains all over it."

Brendan wasn't quite prepared for this up close and personal photo exhibition and Dellanno picked up on it right away. "It appears she was struck from behind by the initial blow, which indicates she was trying to evade her attacker", he went on. "She was struck with great force Brendan. Whoever hit her knew how to put the fat part of the bat on the ball, so to speak. No easy task given that the target was moving at the time."

"Hey, how'd you do against the breaking ball in high school, kid?" Freedman jumped in. "I remember reading you were a pretty good curve-ball hitter."

"What's your fucking fascination with my baseball career, detectives?" Brendan wanted to know. "Yeah, I could hit the curve, no problem. But that doesn't mean I cracked Jacquie's head open, which is what you seem to be implying. I'd like to call a lawyer now. Will you hand me my phone?"

"I don't think that's necessary, Brendan. Let's look through a few more pictures and see where that gets us", Dellanno suggested. "Here's a similar picture from a different angle. Does anything jump out at you as being out of place or unusual in any way?"

"I don't know, I don't think I've ever been inside the Reinhartsen's bedroom before," Brendan informed Bobby. "So I really couldn't tell you."

"What about the garage, Brendan?" Dellanno asked. "Have you ever been inside the Reinhartsen's garage?"

"I have, but what's that got to do with anything?" Brendan wanted to know.

"I'm glad you asked", Dellanno replied. "If you'll take a look at this picture you'll notice that's where Big John met his demise, right there in the garage. He may have been out for a ride and upon returning home was surprised by his attacker as he exited his vehicle. Is there anything about the garage or your father's appearance that strikes you as odd, Brendan?"

"He was *not* my father, at least not in the traditional sense of the word", Brendan retorted. "So why don't you stop referring to him as that? He was a nasty piece of shit and I never liked him or felt comfortable around him. And you're obviously just saying it to fuck with me, so; should I start fucking with you back, detective? Would that be helpful? I'm new at this, that's why I ask."

"Do you notice anything odd in this picture, Brendan?" Dellanno continued without acknowledging Brendan's rhetoric.

"Well, I can't see his face, it's all blocked out for some reason", Brendan said. "How do I even know it's him?"

"You'll have to take our word for it", Dellanno replied. "There's nothing to be gained by showing you a photo of someone else's corpse."

"Why are his fingers crushed?" Brendan wanted to know.

"That's a good question, one we don't have an answer to yet", Dellanno admitted. "Is there anything else you notice about his hands that doesn't make sense?"

"Yeah, he's not wearing his college football ring", Brendan answered without hesitation.

"And why would you notice something so trivial, if you don't mind me asking, *Mr.* McAvoy?" Dellanno pressed.

"Because it's not the least bit trivial, *detective*", Brendan continued. "He used to make me pay homage to that fucking ring every time I was near him. I've never seen him without it. He used to say 'Brendan, you're capable of winning a ring like this, even an MVP award if you keep at it. You've got the skills son – not like that other clown over there'. And he'd point at Johnnie while saying it loud enough for him to hear, just to fuck with him. I guess now I understand why he took such an interest in me."

"Sure seems to make sense", Dellanno agreed. "Is anything else missing or out of place?"

"Not that I can tell", Brendan told the detective.

"OK, give Det. Freedman and me a few minutes. We'll be right back", Dellanno promised. "Can we get you a drink or something while you wait?

"You can get me the fuck outta here and let me go home", Brendan requested. "I've got plenty to drink there."

"Shouldn't be too much longer, son. Hang in there", Dellanno suggested.

But Brendan was having trouble "hanging in there". This situation was feeling more and more dire by the minute.

Johnnie needed to take his mind off of Hayley and had been trying to reach Brendan on his cell phone for about an hour, but to no avail. "Where the fuck is he?" he wondered, his patience wearing thin. "Fuck it", he thought. "I'll just go out by myself. Maybe meet someone new that I can throw in *her* face." But he knew he wasn't going to meet anyone new. He was totally wrapped around Hayley and the alcohol only served to deepen his depression. "Why the fuck would she do this to me? What the fuck did I do to her? It's that fucking cop's fault. That motherfucker is *not* going to get away with this. I should go down to that police station right now and straighten this shit out. In fact, that's exactly what I'm going to do." Johnnie wasn't thinking straight at this point. Going to a police station to "straighten shit out" with a cop who you think is fucking your girlfriend probably wasn't the smartest thing to do, but he was doing it none the less. It seems the more you twist and turn, the more tangled the web gets. But you never notice until it's too late.

Dellanno and Freedman made their way back to the interrogation room after another 20 minutes or so and sat down. Dellanno appeared to be fiddling with something in his left hand. "So, it's a funny thing about that ring", he said. "I had your brother in here a few days ago to look at these pictures and, guess what? He noticed the ring was missing, too. Noticed it right away. When he mentioned it I started to think about why that ring, and only that ring, was taken to begin with. You know, lots of times a murderer will take something off of the victim to keep as sort of a memento. They get some morbid satisfaction, almost a perverse sexual pleasure, out of holding onto the victim's possessions. Pretty sick shit when you think about it, right? If the murderer knows the victim they'll usually take something they know was important to that person if they have the opportunity. Like Big John's ring, for instance."

Brendan was only half listening. His main point of focus was on Johnnie. If he'd been down to the police station to look at these pictures, why hadn't he mentioned it? Did Johnnie point Dellanno in his direction? No way. They were tight. They were brothers. He'd never betray him like this. Plus, he said he didn't think he did it anyway. But if he didn't bring him into it, who did?

He was snapped out of his trance by the sudden sound of metal pinging against metal. When he refocused his attention he noticed a ring sitting on the table, the bright stone setting looking like the eye of a predator, staring straight at him as it slowly moved in for the kill. Then he realized what it was that he was looking at. It was Big John's Syracuse football ring. It couldn't be, yet; there it was.

"You seem surprised to see this, Brendan. Do you know what it is?" Dellanno asked, even though he obviously knew the answer to the question.

"Holy shit! It's Big John's Syracuse ring", Brendan practically screamed. "But where'd you get it?"

"I think you know where we got it, Brendan. Why don't you tell us about it?" Dellanno suggested.

"I've already told you everything I know", Brendan answered. "Big John was super proud of that ring. He never took it off and he always made a fuss over it. There's not much more to tell."

"Are you sure you don't want to add a little more to the story, kid?" Dellanno asked.

"Where did you get this? And why are you talking to me as though I know more than what I've already told you?" Brendan was starting to freak out now.

"Well I thought you might know how it ended up inside your jewellery box alongside your Puka shell necklaces and your cute little 'Brendan' ID bracelets", Dellanno informed him.

"Bullshit! There's no way that ring was inside that box unless you guys put it there", Brendan accused the detectives. "I want a fucking lawyer and I want one now!"

"I'm afraid that's not the case, Brendan", Dellanno corrected him. "And Detective Freedman here can vouch for that, isn't that right, detective?"

"100% correct, detective", Freedman agreed. "That ring was definitely inside that jewellery box when we came across it."

"What do you mean 'when you came across it'?" Brendan wanted to know. "How did you happen to come across it, anyway?"

"Well, when your brother came down to look at the photos of his dead parents, his girlfriend was here with him", Dellanno began to explain. "Apparently, you stored your things in her apartment while you were waiting to move into yours. From what we understand, you took a quick inventory of your belongings and left the jewellery box sitting there, wide open. We got a call from the girl saying she saw what looked like the ring in question sitting inside the open box. Does any of that ring a bell, Brendan?"

"Everything but the part about me leaving the box open", Brendan said. "I don't even remember touching that box as a matter of fact."

"Well you looked through a lot of stuff in a short period of time. I wouldn't expect you to remember every item you put your hand on or moved to another location", Dellanno explained.

"Look, if what you're saying is true, I still don't have the slightest idea how that ring got there", Brendan swore. "This stuff has been sitting in my parent's house for years. Maybe someone else put it there. Maybe it was my father." Brendan stopped himself from saying anything more about Tom.

"Which 'father' are we talking about", Dellanno was wondering.

"Tom McAvoy, the man who raised me. My real father", Brendan said.

"Sure, it would be easy to use Tom as a scapegoat now. After all, he's dead", Dellanno reminded Brendan. "There are no longer any consequences for him, not here on earth, anyway."

"Before he committed suicide, he left me a note", Brendan went on. "In it, he said he had some horrible secret he'd been carrying around for a long time and that he could no longer bear the burden of whatever it was. I thought it was the fact that he was having an affair to get even with my mother, but now I think it might be that he had something to do with those murders."

"We'll need to see a copy of that note, along with anything else in his own handwriting to compare it to", Dellanno advised.

"I burned the note", Brendan admitted.

"Oh, you *burned* the note", Dellanno replied. "That's convenient, isn't it? And what would make you do something like that?"

"I remember thinking at the time that his secret was that he murdered the Reinhartsen's out of revenge or something, and I didn't want anyone else to ever think that, so I burned the note," Brendan explained.

"How tidy is that?" Dellanno asked. "Something that could have potentially helped you no longer exists because a boy loved his father so much he didn't want anyone to think he'd be capable of such a horrendous act. What a great Movie of the Week that would make, Brendan."

"This is so out of control at this point", Brendan sighed. "I did not kill the Reinhartsen's. I didn't kill *anybody*. I have no idea how that ring got there but I know I had nothing to do with it. Maybe Tom wanted me to have something from my biological father so he left it there for me."

"Well, let's bring Tom in for questioning so we can get to the bottom of it – oh, wait; we can't, because Tom's dead", Dellanno deadpanned. "Look kid, all arrows are pointing directly at you for this. You had the motive – revenge and a huge inheritance - you had the opportunity, and, most importantly, you had the ring with the inscription 'Big John R-ange' scribbled inside. Things are not looking too good for you at the momment, Brendan McAvoy. Not good at all. You can call that lawyer now and have him meet us at the Greenwich PD in Connecticut."

*

Johnnie showed up at the station house just in time to
see Brendan being led out in handcuffs. "What the fuck!"
Johnnie screamed. "Why the fuck is my brother in
handcuffs? Where are you taking him?"

"Your brother's on his way to Connecticut, where he'll
be charged with the murder of your mother and father,
John and Jacqueline Reinhartsen", Freedman informed
Johnnie.

"I didn't kill anyone, Johnnie", Brendan told his
brother. "This is total bullshit and your fucking girlfriend
has something to do with it."

"Your girlfriend happened to find your father's
Syracuse football ring in your brother's jewellery box,
which was stored in her apartment and left opened",
Dellanno informed Johnnie. "She called us out of concern
for your life and her own, Johnnie. That's what she's got
to do with it."

"Are you sure she didn't let that slip while you were
fucking her, detective?" Johnnie replied. "Sometimes
people say stupid shit in the heat of the moment."

"I don't know where you got the idea I was fucking
your girlfriend, kid; but you're way off base", Dellanno
lied.

"There's no way Brendan killed my parents. I don't
know how that ring turned up but I know he didn't have
anything to do with it", Johnnie told Dellanno. "And you
can lie all you want about Hayley. I know what the deal is
and so do you. You can have her, for all I give a shit. I just
want you to know that what the two of you have been

doing behind my back is totally fucked up. You're a piece of shit, detective."

"Johnnie, I'm being arrested for murder. Can you deal with your own trivial shit later and get me a good fucking lawyer, like now", Brendan begged his brother.

Johnnie's head was spinning as he walked into his apartment. How was it possible that he lost his girlfriend and his brother, the only two people on the planet he actually cared about, within an hour of each other? And now he had to figure out how to keep his brother from going to jail for something he was sure he didn't do. This was all too much for him to handle. Maybe a joint would help, he thought. It was too late to call anyone anyway. It would have to wait until the morning. So he rolled himself a nice fat one and smoked until his brain turned off.

He was awakened by the sound of the front door opening and closing. Hayley walked in tentatively, not quite sure if Johnnie was up to speed on what was happening to Brendan. She spoke first. "Hey Johnnie", she said in her best little girl voice. "You ok?"

Johnnie wasn't quite sure what she was asking him. Was she asking him if he was ok about what had happened between them, about her fucking that cop? Or was she asking if he was ok about what happened with Brendan, about the fact that she went ahead and did exactly what he asked her not to do, completely fucking up his life?

"Go away", Johnnie said without a hint of emotion. "Get the fuck out of my apartment and get the fuck out of my life. I fucking hate you."

"No you don't, Johnnie. You're just upset", Hayley replied. "And I don't blame you but you have to understand, what I did I did as much for you as for myself. I know you don't think Brendan's dangerous but I disagree. He killed your parents and what's to stop him from doing the same to us?"

"How 'bout the fact that he *didn't* kill my parents?" Brendan asked. "Look, just get the fuck out and leave me alone. We're done. And as far as our little deal goes, forget it. You're on your own now, unless you can get your boyfriend Bobby to support you. You fucked up, Hayley, now you have to pay the price."

Hayley was starting to panic. This is not how she expected things to turn out. With Brendan gone she was supposed to have Johnnie all to herself. Now what the fuck was she going to do? She had no money, no job, and nowhere to go. She needed time to develop a new plan.

She walked over to the couch and sat down close, her legs leaning against his. "Do you think I can stay in the studio until the end of the month, Johnnie?" She asked in her sweet, little girl voice once again. "I've got nowhere else to go." She started tickling his neck with her long fingernails as she waited for his response.

"You've got until the end of the month", Johnnie assured her. "And, during that time, if you see me in the building, or on the street, or anywhere for that matter;

don't say hello. Don't say anything. Now get the fuck out of my house."

Brendan awoke the next morning to the sound of a breakfast tray clanking against the bars of a holding pen somewhere in Connecticut. Johnnie awoke on his couch to the sound of the TV, which had been on all night. Hayley awoke to the silence of her studio, wondering how she was going to navigate the rough waters ahead. Bobby awoke next to his wife, hoping it wasn't too late to salvage what was left of his life. And as they squirmed the webs tightened.

CHAPTER SEVENTEEN

Hayley met Bobby that afternoon at his friend's apartment in Brooklyn Heights. His friend was out of town but Bobby had a key. In spite of everything, or maybe because of it, he was extremely excited to see her. He felt like a teenager with his first real girlfriend. Hayley needed to keep up with appearances, at least until Brendan was officially put away, so she dialled up the charm.

"Strangest thing happened last night", Bobby said. "As Freedman and I were leading Brendan out of the House and to the car, Johnnie showed up. I have no idea why, but there he was, screaming that Brendan didn't kill anybody. Then he launched into a tirade about me 'fucking his girlfriend'."

"What did you say when he said that?" Hayley asked.

"I told him he was way off base", Bobby answered. "I almost said no, I 'made *love* to your girlfriend, there's a difference', but I figured that would have been pushing things a little too far."

"I wonder what he was doing there. He probably went down to confront you", Hayley guessed. "The timing couldn't have been worse."

"Actually, the timing probably worked in his favor. If he wasn't distracted by seeing us with Brendan, things would have ended badly for your boyfriend", Bobby explained.

"My *ex*-boyfriend", Hayley corrected him.

"No shit! What happened?" Bobby asked.

"Well, somehow he knew it was me that led you to Brendan" she said. "And, of course, he's sure we've been fucking, even though I never admitted to it."

"Yeah, Brendan ratted you out to him", Bobby explained. "I tried to ignore the copulation thing."

"Are you still trying to ignore the copulation thing, or is that something we can revisit at this point in time?" Hayley asked, seductively.

"You read my mind, and my little buddy's, too", Bobby replied.

"Well then, why do you still have cloths on, detective?" Hayley wanted to know.

Brendan was handed his cell phone and told he was allowed to make one phone call under the supervision of the guard. He immediately called Johnnie.

"Bro, I'm being held at the State Police barracks in Greenwich. You gotta get me the fuck outta here. I need the best lawyers you can find. I'm talkin' like O.J. Simpson type lawyers", Brendan pleaded with his brother.

"I'm on it, Brendan. Hang tough and we'll get you out of there as soon as possible. Oh, one more thing – who's O.J. Simpson?"

"You're fucking pathetic", was all Brendan could say as he hung up the phone.

*

Hayley and Bobby lay side by side on the bed, once again drenched in sweat. "Holy shit!" Bobby said. "That was off the charts amazing."

"Yeah, I gotta say, that was pretty good for the appetizer" Hayley agreed. "Let me know when you're ready for the entre."

"You trying to give me a heart attack?" Bobby wondered.

Bobby's cell phone rang before she could answer the question. "Shit, I gotta grab this. I hate to ask you this, but could you stay quiet while I'm on?"

"No problem, detective. Do your thing", Hayley advised.

When Bobby hung up, Hayley started talking about Johnnie. "You know, I feel kinda sorry for him, the poor schmuck. He had a horribly fucked up childhood, started to get happy only to have his world cave in on him again. He had to look at grizzly pictures of his dead mother and father – well, at least you spared him the horror of seeing his dad with a bicycle pump shoved halfway down his throat – and then he finds out his brother, whom he had just gotten to know, killed his parents. Not to mention – he believes this really cute cop is now fucking his girlfriend. The poor guy, what a nightmare. Who was that you were talking to just now?"

"That", Bobby said, "was my wife." He was unsure of how Hayley would react to what he had just said given that this was unchartered territory. Gina had never come up in conversation before.

"Oh, your *wife*", Hayley said for dramatic effect. "I was wondering about that. Well, I guess I don't have to wonder anymore."

"Yeah, I suppose I should have mentioned it earlier", Bobby said, apologetically.

"You don't have to worry about me, detective", Hayley promised. "I kinda figured a cute guy like you wasn't going home to an empty house every night."

"Yeah, well; I still should have said something. Ready to go", Bobby asked.

"Let's do it", Hayley replied.

Three or four days had gone by before Bobby spoke with Hayley again. He was busy writing up a sanitized version of the events that led to the investigation and capture of a dangerous killer as well as working his other cases. But that wasn't enough to keep him from thinking about her constantly.

Hayley, on the other hand, was busy trying to figure out what her next move would be. It was dog eat dog; survival of the fittest as far as she could tell and she'd be damned if she were going back to living hand to mouth as a waitress or an Abercrombie clerk. It was time to get serious about her art again. She had the talent, the ambition and the drive. All she needed was a little luck and, she supposed, a new benefactor. She'd seen Johnnie from a distance once or twice and waved to him, certain he'd seen her, but he just looked the other way. Mr. all or nothing.

Brendan was busy strategizing with his lawyers – a $2,500 per hour team of two who were more than happy to spend every minute they could working on the case. They were having a tough time figuring out how to explain the ring in Brendan's possession but they communicated none of that concern to their client. Why worry him? As far as he was concerned he had the best professionals money could buy and it was only a matter of time before he'd have his freedom back.

Johnnie took a car service to Greenwich every other day to visit his brother and cheer him up. But that was challenging for Johnnie because he had little or no cheer to offer. This thing with Hayley really fucked him up. But blood is definitely thicker than water. He was doing the right thing, he told himself.

"Hey Hayley", Bobby said as she answered her phone. "I need to talk to you. I've been doing a ton of thinking about the case this past week and I think I've come up with a way to make sure our killer is convicted beyond a reasonable doubt. Beyond any doubt, for that matter."

"That's fantastic news Bobby!" Hayley told him. "I can't thank you enough for everything you've done. You are a brilliant Detective, sir."

"Not that brilliant, I'm afraid", Bobby said. "There were lots of little things I didn't pick up on along the way. My judgement was clouded – I crossed the line. I violated the number one rule of police investigation: do not become intimately involved with any person or persons connected with the case."

"Well, it's not *all* your fault, Bobby; I think I contributed to what happened", Hayley offered. "I'm just as guilty."

"Yes, I suppose you are", Bobby replied. "Listen, let's meet somewhere out of the neighborhood tomorrow. I really want to run some stuff by you."

"How could I say no?" Hayley replied. "Are we talking Brooklyn Heights or some other clandestine location?"

"I'm afraid my friend is back in town", Bobby said with obvious disappointment. "Why don't we do this – let's meet at Roger's Diner. We can have a bite to eat and take it from there. I get off at 8:00. Shall we say 8:30?"

"Is that A.M. or P.M, officer?" Hayley inquired.

"That would be P.M., Ma'am", Bobby clarified.

"Good, because a girl needs to get her beauty rest. I'll see you there at 8:30, Detective", Hayley promised.

"I can't wait", Bobby replied as he hung up the phone.

Bobby had a hard time sleeping that night. He was feeling incredibly guilty about his enormous error in judgement and knew that he wasn't going to be able to keep it from Gina much longer. It was eating him up inside. He could only hope that when his day of reckoning came she'd find it in her heart to forgive him. This thing with Hayley got out of control so quickly. And Johnnie would surely bring all of it up at trial and he'd have to answer to it. He needed some guidance and he needed it quickly, so he spent a good portion of the next day locked in his Lieutenant's office revisiting every aspect of the case. He and his boss were friends so he left out no detail. He sought his personal advice as well as his professional guidance. He'd fucked up on a grand scale and the conclusion they'd arrived at was that he needed to come clean, both with the department *and* his wife. Having all this shit come out in the courtroom wouldn't bode well for Bobby. So the Lieutenant made a call to a friend in Internal Affairs, someone he absolutely trusted, and asked him to come up to his office as soon as possible, that it was a matter of utmost urgency.

Bobby got to the diner by 7:30. He'd punched out early because he wanted to meet with Roger before Hayley showed up and have him play devil's advocate. Roger was good at that, he could punch holes in anything but even he had to admit Bobby's plan was on the money. He felt certain that if Bobby could pull this off, justice would be served. He walked back into the kitchen just as Hayley was walking through the front door. Bobby waved her over.

"Well, this is romantic", Hayley said facetiously. "A cosy little breakfast diner for dinner."

"I'll have you know", Bobby said, "that you'll not find a better Baba Ganoush anywhere in the 5 boroughs of this city, Miss Mullany. I recommend you eat before you disparage this fine establishment."

"Fair enough", Hayley surrendered. "Where's Roger? I figured I'd find his massive frame taking up half the booth again."

"You just missed him", Bobby said. "He needed to get home before his wife accused him of seeing other women for the fiftieth time this week. Who would do a sleazy thing like that, anyway?"

"I couldn't imagine", Hayley said, removing her shoe and gently messaging his crotch with her bare foot.

"It takes all kinds, I guess", Bobby replied, amazed at how quickly he'd become aroused.

"So, what did you want to talk to me about?" Hayley wondered. "The sooner we get that out of the way, the sooner we can take care of this other rather large issue that sprang up recently."

"I'm glad you asked, Hayley", Bobby said. "I've been thinking and thinking and thinking about this case we've built against Brendan and, while I'm delighted we came across the physical evidence that will almost certainly put him away for the rest of his life, something about the case has been gnawing away at me recently. I couldn't put my finger on it until I reviewed everything start to finish with my Lieutenant this morning. There was just something about Brendan's demeanor and the responses he gave while being interrogated that left me just south of convinced he was our man."

"Yeah, Brendan's got ice running through his veins", Hayley said. "He's as cold-blooded as they come. I'm not surprised he had you doubting yourself, even with the ring and all. He's extremely intelligent and manipulative."

"True, but that's not the part that got me to thinking", Bobby continued.

"So, what did get you to thinking, Detective? Was it something he said or something he did?" Hayley wondered while she continued to work her magic under the table.

"It was actually something *you* said, Hayley", Bobby went on.

"Something *I* said", Hayley asked. "What could I have possibly said that would make you doubt Brendan's guilt? I'm the one that brought him to you to begin with."

"Yes, that's true", Bobby admitted. "But it was something you mentioned in passing, something you just happened to let slip that really struck a chord in me. I couldn't figure it out at first, but then it hit me, and I started doing some extra digging."

"Well let's clear up the confusion right now, detective", Hayley suggested. "If I said anything that led you to believe in any way that Brendan wasn't as guilty as Judas handing Jesus over to the Romans, then I would respectfully ask that we retract that statement immediately. That is one dangerous kid and he needs to be put away."

"If it were only that easy, Hayley", Bobby said. "My brain just doesn't work that way, now that it's actually starting to work again."

"Come on, Bobby. This is starting to get weird", Hayley said. "Tell me what's going on. If Brendan walks free I'm gonna have to go into witness protection."

"When we were at my friend's apartment last week you started talking about Johnnie. You said you felt bad for him after all he'd been through", Bobby reminded her.

"I remember", Hayley said. "Go on."

"Well, in every police investigation there's a critical piece of evidence that the public never gets to see or hear about", Bobby said. "The trick during an interrogation is to try and get the suspect to acknowledge that he has information that only the police are aware of. We try and lead him into telling us something no one else could possibly know about."

"I guess that makes sense", Hayley admitted. "But what's that got to do with you doubting Brendan's guilt?"

"So, before we get to that, I mentioned that I did some extra digging to see what I could come up with", Bobby explained. "One of the things I did was run Big John Reinhartsen's credit cards for the months preceding the murders, just to see if there were any discernible patterns of behavior I could pick up from them. The one thing that stood out clear as day was that Big John was an aficionado of high end strip clubs here in the city."

"What guy isn't?" Hayley wanted to know. "Are you gonna tell me you've never been to a strip club before, Bobby?"

"Sure, for bachelor parties and special occasions", Bobby admitted. "But this guy took it to a whole nother level. I mean he could easily drop ten grand a week in these places, which he often did."

"So, what's that got to do with Brendan", she wanted to know.

"Indirectly, everything", Bobby replied.

"Not sure I follow", Hayley proclaimed.

"Stay with me", Bobby said. "I spoke to half a dozen of these strip club managers over the past few days and each of them remembered that you worked in all these clubs prior to your blacklisting. Do you ever remember running into Big John while you were working?"

"Are you fucking kidding me, Bobby?" Hayley asked, shocked. "I'd do eighty to a hundred dances on a *bad* night. Do you actually think I can remember an individual that happened to come into the club, regularly or otherwise?"

"Well I thought you might remember him because when someone goes into the Champagne room with a girl and puts it on their credit card, the club jots down the name of the dancer on their copy of the receipt", Bobby explained.

"Huh, I did not realize that", Hayley said, surprised. "You learn something new every day."

"Ain't that the truth", Bobby agreed. "Anyway, it seems Big John was a Champagne room regular of yours, Hayley. Your name is all over those receipts, every one of them."

"Well I'm sorry I don't remember him. I'm sure he didn't go by his real name and I had lots of regulars. I was pretty good at what I did, as I'm certain you could attest to, Bobby", Hayley replied.

"I suppose that could be true", Bobby agreed. "And I'd buy it if it wasn't for that one little matter of the evidence."

"Yeah, you still haven't explained that one", Hayley said.

"I was just getting around to it", Bobby assured her. "Remember I said there's always at least one piece of physical evidence that is never released to the public?"

"I remember", Hayley said, impatiently. "Go on."

"Well, with regards to the Reinhartsen murders, it was never released that Big John was found with a bicycle pump shoved down his throat, Hayley", Bobby went on. "When you were talking about how badly you felt for poor little Johnnie, you mentioned how grateful you were he didn't have to see the photo of his dad swallowing that pump. How would you know about that, Hayley, if that was the hold back? That's the thing that was gnawing away at me. At first I thought I might have let it slip at some point, but that's an amateur move, never would've happened. When I realized the only way you could have known about that pump would have been for you to have put it there yourself, I broke out in a cold sweat. Did you stick that bicycle pump down Big John's throat, Hayley?"

"Are you fucking kidding me, Bobby?" Hayley shot back. "Do you really think I'm capable of doing something so horrendous?"

"You tell me", Bobby went on without emotion. "Did you stick that bicycle pump down Big John Reinhartsen's throat, Hayley?"

"Of course not, Bobby; I could never bring myself to do something like that", Hayley swore.

"I'm thinking Jacquie was probably just a casualty of war", Bobby continued. "I'm thinking you never meant to hurt her but she probably heard all the commotion in the garage, came in and got a good look at you finishing off Big John, turned and ran. I'm thinking you caught up with her in her bedroom and had no choice really but to swing the Louisville Slugger as though the game depended upon it. Does that sound about right, Hayley?"

"You're fucking crazy, Bobby", Hayley said adamantly. "I think the stress of this case has gotten to you. Maybe you need a vacation. Take your wife and get outta here for a little while."

"You killed Big John and Jacquie Reinhartsen, took Big John's ring, probably as some kind of morbid keepsake, and then used it to set Brendan up. It couldn't have been orchestrated more brilliantly Hayley, even if it was just a coincidence that you all came together to play a role in this little vignette", Bobby pressed. "Isn't that right, Hayley? Could I *be* any more on the money, *Hayley*???"

"Yeah, that's right *Bobby*, I killed that motherfucker and he deserved it", Hayley conceded. "And you're right about the wife, too; I had no intention of hurting her but she left me no choice. She saw everything. I wasn't about to go to jail for doing the world a favor by removing that scumbag from the planet."

"I see. Now all I need is to understand why, Hayley", Bobby went on in an even tone. Now that he finally had her talking he didn't want to risk distracting her. "What could possibly push you to do something so incredibly horrible, a nice Catholic girl like you?"

"He was a regular customer, Bobby. He was my bread and butter", she explained. "I'd send him a text to let him know where I'd be working and he'd show up without fail. I'd give him a few lap dances to get him going and then it was off to the private room for a few of hours. He'd slip the bouncers a couple of hundred each to look the other way and they were more than happy to oblige. At first he was a little timid, never pushed the envelope, but after a while he started to get more and more

aggressive. He started to get violent with me. I knew I
should have blown the whistle on him then but I needed
the money and he was overly generous in that respect",
Hayley went on with an aloofness in her voice that made it
sound as though she were reading a passage from a novel.
"Then, one night, he forced himself down my throat,
violently, even though I begged him not to. 'Shut the fuck
up, you little bitch' he screamed. 'I'll do whatever the fuck
I want. I fucking *own* you.' He just about choked me to
death with that freak-show cock of his and I vowed that
night that I would get even with him; that he wasn't going
to get away with it. So I waited, about two months. I
began observing his comings and goings, looking for
patterns that would help me figure out the optimal time to
make my move. I had no idea about Johnnie, I mean I
knew he had a son, I just didn't pay much attention to him.
Meeting him in the park that day was a total coincidence. I
almost shit my pants when he told me what his real name
was. I put that together with his bogus story about writing
a novel about the kid who kills his parents and I knew
immediately that God had set this up for some reason. So I
let it play out. Then Brendan shows up and I start
thinking, how easy would it be to set this poor schmuck up
under the circumstances. I mean, I had the ring, all I
needed to do was to figure out a legit way to plant it on
him and he'd be done. Then the incident with the elevator
occurred. It was too easy. And then there was you,
detective. How unexpected that Johnnie would happen
into the club that night and smash that poor bastards face

with a bottle. If that hadn't happened I never would have met you. And what a sucker you've been. You couldn't have made it any easier, Bobby. Everything just fell into place like it was meant to be."

"Why the bicycle pump?" Bobby asked.

"Because I wanted that motherfucker to feel what it was like to have a giant pipe shoved down his throat, over and over again. I even made him beg me not to do it", Hayley explained.

"And the fingers?" Bobby went on.

"I smashed them so the son-of-a-bitch wouldn't be able to hit another woman, ever again", Hayley said.

"Wouldn't the part where you'd killed him already have taken care of that?" Bobby said.

"You can never be too careful, detective", Hayley assured him, as serious as can be.

"Well, that's quite a story, Hayley", Bobby admitted. "You do know what has to happen now, don't you?"

"Yeah, good fucking luck with that, cop", Hayley said in a voice that reminded Bobby of the devil. "It's my word against yours. 'Oh, I'm so sorry to be wasting your time like this, Your Honor. You see, Detective Dellanno used to come into the club all the time asking for me. He was infatuated with me, stalking me all the time. He'd wait outside the club 'til I got off and offer to drive me home. When I told him I wasn't interested in him in that way, he waited for me one night as he'd always done, dragged me into his car and raped me repeatedly. He said that if I ever told anyone, he'd kill me. I was so scared, Your Honor. I was *petrified*! Then he made this whole thing up about me being a murderer to get even with me. He's probably the one that did it. He used to glare at Mr. Reinhartsen whenever he'd see me with him.' Who's a jury gonna believe, Bobby? I'm quite an actress, as you probably know by now. Think about it. I will wreck your life. You'll be fired from your job, your wife will leave you; you'll have nothing, Bobby. You will have *nothing*."

"You're going away, Hayley; and for a very long time. You can count on it", Bobby promised her.

"Dream on, Bobby", Hayley said. "It's *my* word against *yours*. I'll play those odds any day of the week. You know, the easiest thing would be to just keep this conversation between the two of us. Let Brendan take the rap."

"Actually Hayley, it's *your* word against *ours*", Bobby corrected her.

"What's that supposed to mean", Hayley asked. "Are you going all schizoid on me now? You'd better book that little vacation while you still can."

Bobby stood up and opened his shirt. At about the same time she noticed the wires taped to his chest, Hayley noticed the flashing lights outside the diner window. Several men in suits followed by a slew of uniformed police officers entered the diner with their guns drawn and went directly over to Bobby and Hayley. Lt. Burns and Sgt. Simpson, the lieutenant's friend from Internal Affairs, were the first to reach them.

"Nice work, Bobby", the lieutenant said. "We got everything, every word. Miss Mullany, you're under arrest for the murders of John and Jacqueline Reinhartsen of Greenwich, Connecticut. You have the right to remain silent. If you give up that right, anything you say can and will be used against you in a court of law. Do you understand those rights, Miss Mullany?" Lt. Burns asked.

Too late for that now, Bobby thought to himself. She's done. Hayley looked at Bobby as if to say "how the fuck could you do this to me", but instead she just walked away in silence. She, too, knew she had no shot at flirting her way out of this one. Bobby turned and thanked Burns and Simpson for allowing him to redeem himself before handing Simpson his badge. As Bobby walked to the waiting unmarked car he spotted Freedman holding the door open for him. "Nice work, Detective", Freedman said with genuine respect.

"Same could be said for you, Detective. Will you be letting Brendan out this evening?" Bobby wanted to know.

"He's already on his way home, Bobby. He asked me to be sure and thank you for giving him his life back" Freedman said.

"Thanks, Keith, for everything", Bobby said as he ducked to get into the car.

"I'd partner up with you anytime, Bobby. It would be my privilege. Good luck and let me know how things turn out for you", Freedman said.

"Will do, Detective. You'll be the first to know", Bobby replied as the car sped off.

EPILOGUE

Johnnie dreamed about his mother again that night. She was once again sitting on the chaise by the pool only this time she wasn't alone, Big John was with her. The two were the picture of youthfulness and good health. Johnnie recognized immediately that he was dreaming and remembered the conversation he and his mom had previously. But he wasn't expecting to see his dad. He was unsure of how to respond but Big John couldn't have been more gracious and loving. Johnnie felt at peace with himself and the world around him for the first time ever. Then, to his surprise, several others emerged from the pool house to join them. He was startled to see Tom, Laura and Brendan, all smiles and chatting away non-stop.

Johnnie and Brendan embraced in a bear hug as he simultaneously greeted the McAvoy's. "What are you doing here, Bren?" Johnnie asked.

"I suppose the same thing you are, John", Brendan replied. "Are we dreaming?"

"Yeah, we're dreaming alright", Johnnie explained. "I only wish we didn't have to wake up."

"One day you won't have to", Big John informed them. "Unless you want to. As your mom explained the last time you two saw each other, Johnnie; it will be up to you whether or not you want to become human again. This is just a taste of what's to come. But I suspect you both understand you still have a lot to experience in your current incarnations. You've already learned some important lessons about kindness and love. I'm sorry you had to go through such pain and anguish to gain that knowledge, and that we all contributed to it; but you guys set it up that way. We were just acting out our parts, which of course we needed to do for our own spiritual development. Take comfort in knowing you're past the worst of it. You'll still have your share of challenges during this lifetime, but they will pale in comparison to what you've already experienced."

"What about Hayley?" Johnnie wanted to know.

"Hayley chose her own path and is not quite as evolved as the two of you, honey", Jacquie said. "She's still got some tough times ahead. But she'll be ok. We all are, eventually. Now why don't you boys throw on some suits and go for a nice swim before it's time for you to go back."

"Do we have to go back", Brendan asked. "It's so much more peaceful here. Can't we stay a while longer?"

"I'm afraid that's not up to us, son", Tom replied. "But I have no doubt we'll see you again soon. As I've told you Brendan, there's a rhyme and a reason to everything."

"Good to know", the two boys said in unison as they walked toward the pool house with their arms around each other's shoulders like a couple of 12 year olds about to go for a swim on a hot summer's day.

*

Brendan awoke early to find Johnnie already sitting on the couch halfway through his morning medicine, watching an episode of "The Brady Bunch". He sat down and took the joint from his brother's outstretched hand.

"I had the strangest dream last night", he said. "I dreamed we..."

"Shhh!" Johnnie said. "Mike Brady's about to launch into a speech about family unity as Greg and Marcia go at each other over which one will become the next class president. Classic Mike Brady. Marcia's so fucking hot."

"Some things never change. You have serious issues, Bro", Brendan said as he took a deep toke off the joint. "*Serious* issues."

"Whatever you say, Brendan", Johnnie replied without taking his eyes off the screen. "Just remember, there's a rhyme and a reason to everything."

"Fuck me! So, it *was* real?" Brendan asked. "You were there, too?"

"As real as the conversation we're having right now", Johnnie informed his brother. "Don't freak, you'll get used to it. I did, but it takes a while. It comes with the territory. Spiritual evolution. In one sense it's all very real", he explained. "You were functioning on a different level at that moment, on a different plain of existence. You were able to gain access to that realm because your conscious mind was at rest. It's too much for your 'wide-awake' mind to comprehend. You were operating outside of the physical realm. The physical part of the dream is an illusion, Bren", Johnnie went on. "Your brain demands these little tricks in order for it to make sense of things. We *choose* to be born into specific situations because there are challenges specific to our beings that we need to work through. That's the real meaning of 'free will'. It's our *choice* to be human. Once you become human you become exposed to a myriad of circumstances, both good and bad, that are created to help you strengthen the under-developed aspects of your core being. It may all seem random, and it certainly isn't easy, but there *is* a rhyme and a reason to all of it. Like I said, it's about spiritual evolution, Bren; about coming to better know and understand the Creator, the Life Force, whom we typically refer to as 'God'. Being human is a struggle, Bro. It's designed to be. But you need to understand that the more difficult things are for you now, the more gratifying they'll be later. You need to know and understand discordance before you can truly appreciate harmony. It's about balance. But eventually you'll know nothing of pain and sadness. Instead, you'll experience feelings of peace and contentment that are beyond your wildest dreams, just like you briefly experienced last night during the deepest part of your slumber."

"Where the fuck did *that* come from?" Brendan asked his brother.

"You know, I'm not really sure", Johnnie said, toking on the joint. "It's just something I seem to know. And I have a strong suspicion its true. Man, what I wouldn't give to go back to 1973 and take Marcia to that God-damned Westdale High School dance."

"You're fucking pathetic, John", Brendan replied. "Let's order up some food. I'm starving."

"Anything you want on your first day of freedom, Bro", Johnnie said. "Anything you want. Welcome home."

About the Author

JAMES CAPUANO is Senior Vice President for the Markets Division at Thomson Reuters, the global news and information company. Jimmy is also the author of the critically-acclaimed memoir *Beast: A Slightly Irreverent Tale About Cancer (And Other Assorted Anecdotes)*. He lives in Manhattan with his wife Dana and their four children.

Photo by Dana Capuano.

You may also enjoy ...

James Capuano's

BEAST

A Slightly Irreverent Tale About Cancer
(And Other Assorted Anecdotes)

Nothing about cancer is funny – so why did I laugh so hard at James Capuano's personal story about his struggles with Stage 4 colon cancer? Simply put: because it's hilarious. Never one to run away from the truth, his in-your-face account tells it like it is, providing valuable insight into how this disease affects not only the body and the mind, but also family and friends. ... A surprisingly life-affirming tale. **- Susan Sarandon**

I … walked away crying, with tears of sadness and laughter. No mean trick. ... A memoir both tender and hard for the healthy and the sick. **- David Duchovny**

… Harrowing, hilarious, heartbreaking, and, most of all, human. I loved it! **- Peter Farrelly**

Available in paper, digital and audio editions.

newstreetcommunications.com

Made in the USA
Lexington, KY
06 September 2014